AROUND A MINNESOTA CAMPFIRE

◁ • ▷

Around a Minnesota Campfire

◁ • ▷

Spooky Tales Told in Minnesota's State and County Parks

Ruth D. Hein

NORTH STAR PRESS OF ST. CLOUD, INC.
St. Cloud, Minnesota

Credits

"Casper's Closet," "Someone Was Jumping on Me," "Fredrica May Have Moved to Fisher," and "A Ghostly 'Coon-Hunting Story," authored by Ruth Hein, have been previously published in *Ghostly Tales of Iowa* by Adventure Publications, copyright 2005.

Published by
North Star Press of St. Cloud, Inc.
P.O. Box 451
St. Cloud, Minnesota 56302
northstarpress.com

‹ • ›

Contents

≺ · ≻

Introduction

Minnesota is blessed with a wealth of fine campgrounds. From small private camps to well-maintained KOAs to amazing state parks, the state has it all. Over the years I've spent a lot of time at these places, and I've learned one thing for certain. Despite what wonders the campground or state park offers during the day, no matter what kind of fishing, swimming, hiking, or wildlife viewing opportunities are available, at night the focus of everyone's attention is the campfire. And there's something about campfires that brings out the ghost stories. Maybe it's the deep darkness all around, the pressing in of nature and night and the wildlife that roams woods and field. Maybe it's the primeval memory of early people sitting on logs around fires, trying to explain a complicated universe. I don't know, but whatever it is, it brings out stories.

Another wonderful thing about Minnesota's amazing campgrounds is that it draws people from pretty well all over the United States, and those nighttime campfires pull in stories that happened thousands of miles from Minnesota soil but that fit around Minnesota campfires comfortably. And, when people hear that I write ghost story books, all the stops are pulled. Ghost stories tumble out, and I scribble them down as well as I can in the uncertain light of the campfire.

For example:

A woman, I'll call her Paula, volunteered something that had happened to her.

Paula said that early one morning, just a couple of weeks after her husband's death, she heard her telephone answering system start up, relaying the message common to many systems: "We're not able to answer the phone right now. After the beep, please leave your name, number, and a brief message." Not just once, though. She heard the answering machine's spiel over and over and over, and, of course, it was programmed only to deliver the message once for each call, and she hadn't had any calls. Paula said she never did figure out why this happened, and she had no idea whether someone was trying to leave a message and couldn't handle the system, or what.

During the day, this would be described as some kind of technical glitch, an annoyance maybe, and Paula should contact the answering machine company. But told at night, this same mechanical problem takes on surreal overtones that have nothing to do with wiring or a little plastic box.

Then Paula said that her apartment had a security system that buzzed into the manager's living quarters when triggered. Paula said, "One morning not more than a day or two later, the system started buzzing at 5:30 in the morning and kept on buzzing probably at least for an hour. I was asleep, but I finally heard the noise and got up to see what was going on. After checking my door and looking around, I disengaged the alarm in my condo, and the racket stopped. When the manager finally woke up, he checked the doors and windows because the lights signaled that the problem was there. He found nothing amiss."

When I told Paula some of the reasons ghosts hang around, according to the book *Things That Go Bump in the Night*, she said, "There definitely was some unfinished business then, though I don't know what it was." She thought maybe her late husband came back and caused the otherwise unexplainable happenings as a way of checking up on her, seeing if she were okay. Everyone listening to her story agreed.

Paula said, "I do talk to him and tell him I'm doing all right, that everything's working out but that I still miss him and things like that."

Her story raised goose bumps on everyone's arms, and no one doubted what had happened. But what *had* happened? A couple bits of technology had acted up.

Stories like Paula's never really sound right told in city parks, cafes, or on buses. They sound pretty silly there, almost embarrassing. And they should never be told during the day. Daylight has a way of changing things, explaining everything, but maybe not exactly getting to the truth of anything. Something about night and fire makes it easier for people to open up, to tell what they feel is going on, even if daylight reality disagrees. Sure, there could be a short or glitch in Paula's answering machine and in her alarm system. Stuff like that happens all the time, right? But what are the chances that two different systems go haywire at the same time and both so quickly follow her husband's death? That's a bit too coincidental for my taste.

In my mind, the campfire explanation is the better one, even if it is a bit spooky. Her husband was checking up on her. That's nice. That gave Paula a connection with him, maybe eased her in mourning his death. It certainly gave her more comfort than believing her electrical system was on the fritz.

But what was the truth? We'll never know.

◄ 1 ►

Gift Horse, Ghost Horse

I was sitting at a rather nice campfire in Father Hennepin State Park. It was Memorial Day weekend, and the campgrounds were full. People had boated all day on Mille Lacs Lake, fished and waterskied and toured the big lake. The nice swim beach had been filled with families from all over the state and elsewhere, and the fragrance of barbeques had wafted through the campgrounds towards dark. With dark, the happy laughter of children and chatter of many groups of people settled down to almost a wilderness quiet, and the sparks kicked up by my campfire were only topped by the sea of stars overhead. It was a lovely, gentle evening, but I knew this was Minnesota, and dark would bring out mosquitoes. I took my final walk to the restrooms before turning in. It was on that walk when I struck up a conversation with a couple also on the way to the restrooms. As we waited our turn, we chatted. In short order, I joined them at their fire for a bit of talk. These folks, Gloria and Joel, were visiting Minnesota from Montana and had a very interesting story to tell.

Katelyn, their daughter, had received a horse as a gift from Glennis, a family friend. It wasn't a real, live horse, but a beautiful, large wonder horse—a rocking horse with springs. When batteries were put in place in its belly, it would make the sounds of a horse galloping and neighing. When Katelyn, about a year and a half when she received the gift, rode it very hard for a short while, galloping noises would start. Katelyn loved that toy horse.

At the time the horse was given to their daughter, Gloria and Joel lived in a double-wide trailer in the small town of Hardin, Montana.

1

Gloria said, "Hardin is sixteen miles from the site of the Battle of the Little Big Horn, or as some people call it, Custer's Last Stand."

Perhaps this is as good a time as any to mention that Glennis, their friend, had come by the horse because it was left in the house she rented from a divorced couple. It was the only thing they had left behind in the house. Glennis thought it was a little strange to abandon such a pretty and an unusual toy. She thought maybe they just hadn't had room for it when they moved. Not wanting to give it away if they came back for it, Glennis waited a whole year before she gave it to Katelyn.

The horse was placed in Katelyn's room, of course, a very natural place for it. But before long, things began to happen that weren't so natural. "One weekend when Joel was home alone," Gloria said, "he heard a wind-up toy playing by itself. Then, while he listened to try to identify which toy it was, he heard the horse making the galloping sounds. When he checked the room, no one was there and everything was quiet and still.

"But the sounds continued," Gloria said. "Wind-up toys played by themselves when no one was in the room. We began to find that unexplainable things were happening in the living room as well. For example, our beloved cocker spaniel would have all the hair on her back standing up as she faced the gray chair in the living room corner—the chair that had been her favorite napping place for years. No one was in the chair during those times, yet she barked and growled at the empty chair for no reason apparent to us."

During the summer a few years later, the family moved from town to a mile out into the country. Of course, they moved all Katelyn's toys with them. During the fine weather of the summer the rocking horse sat on the front porch. That fall, they brought it back into the house.

Gloria noticed some things missing from their places in the house, and she heard specific sounds in the night. One was like a marble being slowly bounced down the stairs. Perhaps that was one of the reasons she made sure the doors were locked and secured, chains and all, before they all went to bed. But, when she heard the marble on the stairs and got up to check, nothing was there. Once when she walked into the living room after hearing the marble, she found the front door open. That was spooky, because the chain had been removed.

"When that happened," Gloria said, "because I was the type of person who liked a good ghost story, I concluded we must have a ghost! Others considered that too far-fetched. No one believed what I felt was true. No former residents of the house had experienced anything similar."

In January, the family moved back into town. The house they bought was big enough for the family to grow in. Again, the horse moved with them and was placed in the dining room. DeLaney was born while they lived there.

Gloria said, "We had gotten used to the toys playing, the galloping sounds, and the marbles on the stairs. I stopped moving things back into places when I discovered that, if I left them alone, they ended back on their own. But, something different happened in this new house. In our first week in the house, I heard a child crying. Thinking it was DeLaney, I went upstairs to check on her. Neither she nor Katelyn had awakened. Then we started hearing wind-up toys playing in DeLaney's room when no one was in there with her, and she was way too young to wind them.

"When summer came and the horse was set outside along with other toys, the weird happenings stopped without anyone thinking much about them. But, again, something unfamiliar began, and it was very interesting. DeLaney, almost two then, acquired an imaginary friend. Not another child, though, according to DeLaney. She said the 'friend' was 'big like you' and lived in DeLaney's room. Her name was Brittany. DeLaney was often deep in conversation with Brittany as she played in her room during the day, but she didn't want to sleep in there.

"DeLaney was three when we visited an uncle shortly before Christmas. When DeLaney looked around the room in his home, she very matter-of-factly said, 'Linda isn't here.' Linda, an aunt, had died twenty-one years earlier. We were all taken aback. How could our young daughter even know about Linda? But DeLaney started to talk more about her, and she wanted to talk to Grandma Hardy one night. DeLaney was so serious about it that I called her grandparents up. DeLaney said, 'Linda died.' I asked her how she knew that, but she wouldn't say. She did tell us that she wasn't supposed to talk about Brittany. To us, this was getting rather confusing and mysterious.

"During Christmas vacation, Joel and our girls went ice skating. I stayed home to take a relaxing bath. The tub was filled and ready when

I went to the kitchen to get something to drink. I heard giggling. I had forgotten that I was alone. I went back to the bathroom and found the water splashing about in the tub, but, of course, no one was there. Believe me, I got a chill.

"In January, Katelyn had two friends sleep over. The next day, they were playing upstairs while I was downstairs watching TV and working on a jigsaw puzzle. At one point, I thought I'd go up to check on the girls. I got up and turned the TV off and headed for the stairs. The TV came back on. I turned it off again, and it came back on again. I called the girls down, and all four of us watched. As soon as I turned it off, it came on. We even changed channels, turned it off, and saw it come on. We did this about four times. Then we left it on, and it stayed on. At least, I thought, this time I can tell Joel that I had witnesses!

"So far, most of the unexplainable incidents had been fairly mild. Between that January and March of the following year, things started popping! The toys played more often in the rooms, and every night we heard running upstairs. Then it became obvious that something or someone was pushing Katelyn down the stairs every now and then. She was getting scared.

"One night, our dog, Wolly, stood up in the family room and barked at a brightly lit corner. He refused to go near the area, though. I tried to put him outside, but he wouldn't walk past that part of the room. We were all there, but we couldn't see anything that would spook the dog that badly. After about forty-five minutes, he calmed down, just as if the spirit, or whatever, had left. I don't know . . . maybe he also had felt the chilly breeze we sometimes felt when these things happened.

"In our bathroom we have an old corner hutch, with bottom drawers that we have to pull on, hard, to open. Still, it never tips over. One evening, Katelyn screamed from the bathroom. She was pinned. The cabinet had fallen over her as she crouched low on the floor. The door of the hutch had swung open, and the glass, hitting the sink, had broken into jagged pieces. I had to lift the hutch up and to the side to get Katelyn out from under it. She was crying and quite scared.

"I had Katelyn show me over and over how it had happened. I just couldn't believe that it just fell over. That was when I started thinking that maybe our friendly little spirit was not so friendly anymore.

"One night a little later, Joel was attending a class, so just the girls and I and one of Katelyn's friends, who was staying overnight, were home. I was baking cinnamon rolls. While they were in the oven, smoke started rolling out. I opened the oven door. There was a fire, though nothing had spilled over. I closed the door, and flames shot out of the sides and front of the oven. It was very scary.

"The girls ran upstairs. Katelyn called her Grandpa Hardy. He said to throw water on it. Joel's father came over. He was sure something had spilled in the oven, but he soon found out that nothing had. When Joel got home later that evening, he took the bottom out of the oven. He found nothing at all on the element, nothing burned or scorched, no smoke film. It was clean.

"I haven't mentioned it yet, but we had all gotten used to the phone ringing all the time, with no one there when we answered it. And we were accustomed to hearing footsteps, even running, every night. When Joel knew it wasn't our pets making those sounds, even he admitted that he heard the footsteps. We got used to Katelyn's falls down the stairs. She was so very careful, but still she fell, as if she was pushed down those last few steps. And we began to talk about the chilly breezes as if they were cold spots, where the spirit entered or left the room.

"I had always felt that the spirit in our home was that of a small child, maybe a girl that wanted to live with us, and that DeLaney could see and talk with her, but now I was getting afraid. I read some articles about the real ghostbusters. Every family that reported a ghost or some kind of spirit had reported some of the same happenings: phone calls, a feeling of being pushed, the TV being turned off and on, lights going on or off by themselves, always the footsteps, and sometimes a cool area or cold spot.

"Only once did I see an apparition. It was during the Christmas season, so I had a musical Santa Claus playing. From the corner of my eye, while I stood at the sink doing dishes, I saw a beautiful girl coming to look at the musical Santa. I thought, finally I get to see it! But when I looked over my shoulder in that direction, she quietly moved backwards and just disappeared.

"It was time to bring this all together and either end it or, if we couldn't, at least understand it. Joel and I were working at an Indian

Catholic school on the Crow Reservation. I talked with the priest and one of the nuns about our ghost. They were both of the opinion that the spirit was friendly but might have had unfinished business.

"I took the sister's advice. When I felt by the cool breeze that the spirit had entered the room, I said, 'I don't mean to harm you, but it's time for you to move on and leave us alone, or else to show me what you want us to do for you.' The breeze disappeared when I said that, and I felt calm and at peace again.

"Maybe there were two spirits. Maybe the second was of a different nature and source. We checked with the people who lived in the house before we did, but the only common factor was the rocking horse. I began to wonder why it had been left behind.

"The sister suggested that we should get that horse out of the house. We put it out in a shed. Everything calmed down—the noises in the night, the moving things, the dog's panic attacks—all of it.

"I'm still spooked when I see the horse in the shed. I wonder if it, or an evil spirit somehow existing in it, caused the divorce of the couple who had left it in Glennis's house. It might have—because, while it was in our home, we experienced friction between us and irrational behavior and didn't know why. I remember feeling jealousy and paranoia without knowing its cause.

"It all sounds far-fetched, but telling what happened to us helps a little. We are an educated family, and we believe in God. We weren't looking for a ghost. It just happened to find us, I guess. Or maybe we just happened to be in the right place for it, at the right time. But it was the wrong place for us, as far as I'm concerned, and I'm certainly glad it's moved on."

◄ 2 ►

Nannie May Have Stayed

I was camping at Big Stone Lake State Park on the Minnesota-South Dakota border. This big lake, a remnant of the pre-historic Lake Aggassiz, offered good views of water birds, including pelicans, which I had not seen before outside of Florida. I was intrigued and had watched the pelicans most of the afternoon. During the day, I met a lovely couple, Rick and Laurie from Mitchell, South Dakota. Toward evening, they were walking through the campgrounds and stopped in for a few minutes at my campfire. They told me about a strange happening in Mitchell, South Dakota.

Rick said, "We bought a house two doors down from a massive, four-story brick house whose owners and occupants had always been affluent. A new family with kids my daughter's age moved into that big house on the corner. No one had told them about the ghost that also lived there.

"At the time, since we were new to the neighborhood also, I didn't know about the ghost, either," Rick said, "until their kids and my daughter got together, and the stories started to surface."

Rick began to tell what happened. The new owners were remodeling the house, and the parents spent the night in the room designated for their youngest daughter. In the middle of the night, they woke up to what they described as a cold draft. They felt a "strange sensation, but, of course, they saw nothing," Laurie said.

Another unexplainable incident occurred about a year later. The wife called her husband at work. She said, "You probably won't believe me, but our son's favorite baseball card just flew across the room from the top of the dresser."

To keep from frightening the kids, they blamed it on the wind, but they themselves felt otherwise. That feeling strengthened after they met a former owner of the house. They asked him if he had ever experienced any strange happenings while he lived there.

"Well, he had," Rick said with a smug smile.

The former owner confided, "We always thought the house was haunted by a friendly spirit. We thought it was the ghost of the nanny who was the loyal caretaker of the children of an earlier family. 'Nannie,' as the children called her, had lived in that room and died there of natural causes. We assumed she was still lingering, tending to her duties."

Rick provided more details. "The current family's youngest daughter slept in that same room, and though my daughter frequently stayed overnight with their daughter in that room, we never heard of anything unusual happening there. At least, we weren't told of anything." He added, "We didn't talk about it much because of the kids."

After that family moved to another town, a young, professional couple bought the house. Not long after they moved in, she got pregnant and in due time they brought home a new baby who from then on slept in the crib in that same room.

Rick said that the new parents kept all toys and stuffed animals out of the baby's crib, though dozens of stuffed toys were scattered about in the rest of the room. He said, "Crib deaths were big in the news then. The new parents agreed to keep all the toys out of the baby's crib to eliminate any danger of choking or suffocation."

Late one afternoon, the mom came home from work and went upstairs to wake little Emmaline. She was napping soundly, but all the stuffed animals had been neatly placed around the inside of the crib.

Since the mom's husband was minding things at home, the woman felt he was responsible. She carefully removed the toys from the crib before she went down to confront her husband with the question, "Why did you violate our agreement?"

His answer surprised her. He said, "I just checked her a few minutes before you came home. Everything was in its normal place, and none of the stuffed toys were in the crib!"

"Not long after that," Rick said, "business called them to another location, and they moved. The house was empty when we sold our house and moved to a new neighborhood across town. We drove by there later on, and saw new owners in the house. We've met them, briefly, but I have no idea if they've seen or experienced Nannie, or if they know about her. But how natural it would be for her to be hovering in that room where she lived earlier when she took care of the children of the household. How like her to gently and carefully make the crib cozy for other babies by surrounding them with their own cuddly stuffed animals."

⊰ 3 ⊱

Casper's Closet

While camping at Myre Big Island State Park on Albert Lea Lake near Albert Lea, Minnesota, I encountered Doug and Linda Hill from Decorah, Iowa, who had come up to fish the big lake and camp for the weekend. We met on the beach and had exchanged pleasantries. In the course of our casual conversation, they asked what I did. I told them I was a writer, and it soon came out that I had a passion for ghost stories. They joined me at my campfire that night to fill me in on one they had experienced while living in their first house.

Doug and Linda Hill had lived in a white two-story, four-bedroom home in a new addition at the edge of Grinnell, Iowa. There were no large trees around it to "scritch against the windows . . . nothing to make it spooky," Linda said. They were the first occupants. They had a two-year-old daughter named Erin and were expecting their second child in the fall.

When the events began, they had just returned home from the funeral of a relative in Clarion. Once home, with Erin tucked in, Doug and Linda realized how tired they were, so they also went to bed and were sleeping soundly when something woke them. They both heard three loud knocks . . . not at the outside doors, but on their bedroom wall. Both of them sat up in bed so quickly that they almost knocked each other out as they simultaneously asked, "What was that?"

Between their room and the nursery, all ready for the new baby's arrival, was a closet. It was just an ordinary closet, where they kept their personal, everyday clothing. When they realized the knocks had come from inside the closet, they got out of bed to check it out but could find nothing unusual. No clothing was out of place. Everything seemed to be in order, so they went back to bed.

Over the next several weeks, however, they were awakened out of sound sleep . . . and more than once. Each time, they heard three loud knocks coming from the closet. When they told friends about it, they were told it was probably just the fall weather or the heating system or the plumbing. They were told, "You know the walls can crack when the temperatures change," or, "We've had that happen. It's in the heating system or the plumbing."

But Linda said, "We knew it wasn't. This was something very specific, unique. It didn't come from the water wall next to the bathroom, and it wasn't an outside wall, so there was no reason for it to crack from cold."

They drew the conclusion that a ghost had come to stay with them and was making its presence known with the loud knocking. Linda said, "We called him Casper, the only name we could think of for a friendly ghost. And though we didn't appreciate being awakened in the middle of the night, Casper was never naughty or mischievous, so we were never really afraid. We just accepted him and went about our business."

One night shortly before their son Ryan was born, Linda was having trouble sleeping. She said, "I went downstairs to read awhile so Doug could get a sound night's sleep. From all the way downstairs, I heard the three loud knocks again. I knew it had to be Casper and that he wanted me to hear him. It was as if he was getting serious, although about what, I'm sure I don't know. Doug came running down to see if I'd heard the noise, too. I had, and we sat up together.

"About a week later, Ryan made his entrance into our lives, and we brought home the fourth member of our family. For a while then, with a new baby and a two-year-old to take care of, we were too busy to worry about ghosts.

Doug said, "Remember that Ryan's nursery was right next to our bedroom, and what we dubbed 'Casper's closet' was between the two. As most babies do, Ryan often awoke in the night and cried for attention. A couple of months later, we suddenly realized that we hadn't heard Casper for quite a while. All we could figure out was that he got tired of listening to the crying baby and had decided to go somewhere less noisy to live.

"We haven't experienced anything else that we couldn't explain in some rational way, since that time. So, although we haven't had a ghost since then, we still think back fondly on Casper's stay with us. In fact, we sort of miss him. We find ourselves wondering where he is, who he is haunting now, and whether he'll ever come back to us.

"We left the house in Grinnell and moved to Cedar Rapids when Ryan was in second grade. Later, we moved to Decorah. Casper didn't follow us. At least, all the knocks we've heard since then have been either at the front or the back door, made by people we didn't have to make up a name for."

And, since they were the first occupants of the Grinnell house, they wondered how the house could have had a ghost. No one had died there, which is sometimes given as a reason for the presence of a ghost. I suggested something must have happened on the land before the house was built. Maybe there had once been a claim shanty or a log cabin on the site in the days of early settlement. But they had seen no evidence of an earlier home there. And if the builders or other occupants in that new addition had, Doug and Linda hadn't heard about it. As Linda said, "We just accepted Casper. We were too busy with our young family to worry about him."

⊰ 4 ⊱

Spirits, But Whose?

Ghost stories always attract attention. While Doug and Linda told me about the thumping Casper, other people at nearby camp sites had been listening in. Carla, a lovely woman who was camping with her family, brought a plate of s'mores and sat with us. She had her own story to tell.

Carla started her story by saying, "My mother died in November as a result of an accident. Shortly after she died, my son, Luke, said, 'I saw Grandma standing at the foot of my bed.' He said that several different times. Not long after that, strange things started happening.

"Luke was spooked over his grandmother's appearances," Carla told us. "I tried not to make a big deal out of it. I joked with him and told him to just tell the ghost, 'Knock it off—it scares me!' Luke did that, in a comical way. He told the ghost, 'Why don't you just leave me alone. I'm scared! Go pick on Mom, but don't do that kind of thing around me.' I said, 'Thanks a lot, Luke!'

"Apparently the ghost did as it was asked. Not long after, a couple of my friends came over to my house. We were in the living room. I was sitting on the love seat with Jerry, chatting with Dave, who was sitting on the couch. The couch faced the dining room and kitchen. Around the corner, on the left wall of the dining room, We had a shelf with some glass mugs on it. While we were sitting in the living room, Dave noticed one of the mugs suspended in mid-air for a few seconds. It was almost as if someone was holding it there. When the ghost or whatever it was noticed that we were watching, it let the mug fall to the floor. Surprisingly, it didn't break! We were all a little perplexed. We couldn't even see how it could happen naturally.

"A little later, when Jerry got up and went to the bathroom, Dave and I continued talking in the living room. Jerry came back chuckling. He asked, 'All right, which one of you smart alecks was knocking on the bathroom door?' Dave said, 'Not me,' and I said, 'We were sitting right here. We never moved.'

"Then I said to Jerry, 'You're just shook up because the mug was in the air.' He said, 'No, that wasn't it. Someone was knocking to get in. I figured it was one of you guys, goofin' around.' We finally convinced him it wasn't either of us.

"Later, Jerry was still baffled over the knocking on the door. He and I looked out into the kitchen at the same time. I knew what I saw, but I wasn't going to say anything, so I kept quiet. But Jerry spoke, and you could tell by the look on his face that something had really scared him. I asked, 'What's wrong?' Jerry said, 'I saw a shadow walking right through the cupboards and out of the house.' I had seen it, too. Exactly that.

"The next day when Luke was in the kitchen, the dustpan, which had been lying flat on top of the garbage can, stood up on its edge and flipped over onto the floor. Luke said he hadn't bumped it.

"The following weekend, Jerry came over to stay for the night. We went to bed. When we turned the lights off, we could hear a radio, like a rock station. When we turned the lights on, the music stopped. Just to make sure, I kept turning the light on and off. As fast as the music started with the light off, it stopped with the light on. I thought someone might be watching us from a car outside, trying to spook us with the radio. I decided to get up and look out. I went downstairs. Jerry decided to join me because, though he would be the last to admit it, he was scared and didn't want to be alone. Together we looked all over the house and outside. No car was parked in the driveway or on the street, and none were going by. We found no radio, and the neighbors all appeared to be asleep . . . no music coming from their homes . . . so we decided maybe we were hearing things. We went back to bed and turned the light off. The music started again. We turned the light on. The music stopped. I decided to just listen to the music anyway and try to go to sleep. I was tired, and we were both pretty puzzled, even frightened.

"I was baffled by these strange things happening in the house, so I looked for someone to explain them without telling me I'd lost my mind. I knew I had a letter somewhere from a person who had helped others in similar situations. I called him and told him about the weird happenings. I told him my whole story. I asked, 'Can we find out if it is a ghost, and if so, whose? I'm scared.' He asked if there had been anyone close to me who had died. I said, 'Yes, my mother.' He asked if the things that happened would be things she would do, like leaving the dustpan lying on the garbage can. I told him that Mother wouldn't do that. She always put everything back where it belonged after she used it. Then he asked about my friends, Jerry and Dave. He asked if either of them could be someone Mother would disapprove of.

"I realized that my father, who had died earlier, might not have approved of Jerry, and I thought maybe my mother, so recently deceased, may have felt the same way.

"The man I talked to on the phone said, 'Ghosts are called spirits.' He said my story seemed simple to him. He believed the spirit in my house was that of my mother. For example, the dustpan falling to the floor was her way of saying 'Put this away.' He also thought she disapproved of Jerry a great deal.

"While I was on the phone, the man asked me to say a prayer with him. I asked, 'What good will that do? I pray all the time, but strange things still happen to me. Why would this prayer be any different?' He said, 'This is a prayer to bind the spirit.' I did say a prayer with him then, in my house, over the phone. He told me that things would now be better. He also sent me a list of helps, making use of prayers for spiritual welfare.

"After that, nothing else happened for a while, until one time when I heard a door open upstairs. The upper story of my house had hardwood floors. There's a storeroom up there with a swollen door that, with rain fall humidity, scrapes the floor when it opens. I heard that distinctive sound from downstairs, the door of the storeroom opening. I didn't know what to think. I was alone in the house again, and downstairs. I was scared. When my husband came home from work, we checked the storeroom door together, and it was indeed open.

"About two weeks ago, I was in the living room watching TV. My husband had the second shift from 2:00 p.m. until midnight, and

Luke was at a friend's house, so I was alone in the evening except for our two dogs. While I was watching TV, I heard what sounded like the cough of a young child. I didn't recognize the voice. It was raining steadily outside, so I was sure it didn't come from any child playing out there. Luke was gone, and I knew it wasn't my dogs.

"I told someone about this, and she asked if there had been a suicide, a child dying or anyone losing a baby in the house. I said, 'Yes, I lost a baby last June in this house.' I don't know if that's what caused what I heard . . . if it could possibly have been the spirit of the baby, or what. There had also been other deaths in my family besides my mother, including the unexpected death of a relative who was close to me and protective of me. But most of these happenings that I couldn't explain or even understand took place in the early 1990s, within a few years of Mother's death.

"Someone told me that others with similar experiences had spoken to a spirit, saying, 'I'm fine. You don't need to be here' and sometimes the spirit left. I was ready to try that, but I also wondered if it might be nice to let Mother's spirit, if it was hers, stay around to keep me company in those hours when I was usually alone.

"I've told Ray about all this. He questioned what I told him I had seen and heard. Our friend Dave and my son, Luke, have verified my stories to Ray, and he's beginning to want to get out of our house. In fact, we're both thinking about looking for another place to live . . . a place where we hope the spirit won't find us."

◄ 5 ►

Someone Was Jumping on Me

That's nothing," said Craig, another Iowan who had heard the tones of our ghost stories and wanted to share with us his own tale.

"Thirteen-oh-eight Fifth Street doesn't sound very ominous, does it?" Craig said. "It was my family home, even. I had come home for the week to study for finals, staying in my old room in the basement. With not much else going on other than studying, it was generally a pretty dead week in that quiet town not far from the center of Iowa. Even the two family dogs kept quiet most of the time. But then, unexpectedly, something strange happened to upset the peace and quiet—at least, for me, and maybe the dogs.

"I was suddenly awakened by someone shaking me. At first, I thought that it was my younger brother and his friend pushing on the waterbed mattress. But then I realized I was pressed down into the waterbed and could hardly move. I threatened them. At least, I threatened who I thought it was, in no uncertain terms.

"No one answered me. When I opened my eyes, I saw nothing. Puzzling. I couldn't move. A weight rested on my chest and had pushed me deep down into the mattress. It felt as if someone had been jumping on me, and then stayed there, adding their weight to mine. In that moment of fright, I called out for my Grandmother Evie to help me.

"I really don't know why Grandma Evie came to mind. She had passed away a number of years earlier after a bout with cancer. Still, I found myself calling out for her to help me. I must have sensed her presence watching over me as she had done when I was small. I called out to

17

her rather loudly, and the shaking and the feeling that someone had jumped on me and was sitting on my chest stopped.

"I got up and went upstairs. I saw a red, glowing mass for just an instant between the dining area and the living room. It had no particular shape. The dogs were behind me, barking, when I went through the patio doorway into the screened-in porch and out onto the deck. There was no one outside, and I could see nothing to account for what had just happened inside. When the dogs came out onto the screened-in porch, they quit barking.

"I didn't go back into the house for about an hour. Then I decided that whatever it was, the incident was over. But I never did figure it out. Even thinking it all through again, I don't have a clue. I just know I don't want anything like it to happen again.

"I packed my bag and went back to Ames to study. It took over a year for me to get over the feelings of fright and insecurity I had felt down there in my room in the basement at home. I had recurring nightmares over it for some time afterward.

"Later on, a friend said, 'Craig, when I slept on the couch downstairs in your house, the same sort of thing happened to me.'

"I didn't want to take the chance of going through that experience again, so I sort of fortified myself for anything like it, whenever I slept downstairs at home again, so I can't honestly say that it ever happened to me again. I'm glad of that. That first time shook me up enough!"

⊰ 6 ⊱

Fredrica May Have Moved to Fisher

About this time, I hauled out some research I had been doing into references in Iowa State University publications and in Ames city newspapers leading me to believe that there was a ghost in the university's theater buildings. My research indicated that the ghost may have formerly occupied Shattuck Theatre and moved into the new Fisher Theatre when Shattuck was demolished.

Shattuck was originally built on the Ames campus in 1900 as a stock-judging pavilion. It was a gray, round, frame structure located near the Landscape Architecture and the Journalism buildings. In 1931, when the building was redone, it became the home of the Iowa State Players and was used as a theater workshop until 1973 when Fisher Theatre was ready for use.

Iowa State Players had been established by Fredrica V. Shattuck shortly after she came to ISU in 1914 as the first director of theater on campus. At first, the building was called the theater workshop. Articles state that it was not easy to establish dramatics in the technical school, but Fredrica worked enthusiastically to do just that.

In 1960, the building was renamed Shattuck Theatre in her honor. She had retired in 1948 and had died in 1969. That's when folks on the campus and in the theater say strange things began to occur.

Professors who had directed plays and students who performed in them or helped with sets and lighting were not happy to hear that Shattuck would be torn down, but it was deteriorating, and restoration would be too costly. Perhaps they were not the only ones who would miss it. It seems that, although the students could work there on productions with very little supervision, they hesitated to be there alone at night. They thought the building had a ghost.

Articles from the Special Collections/Archives of the Iowa State University Library relate numerous instances of encounters with a ghost in the stock-judging, pavilion-turned-theater. One student reported outside doors opening on a snowy evening when all the doors were locked. Then came the sound of footsteps followed by a door closing. But there were no tracks out in the snow other than that student's own footprints as he had entered.

Sherry Hoopes, a former ISU speech professor who had also directed several plays, took part in a seance in the theater. Though nothing else noteworthy happened, the group all had the feeling that someone was watchng them.

Students rehearsing late one night heard sounds above them on the stage. When they went up to check, they saw a wheelchair roll across the stage to center and come to a halt facing the audience, in monologue position. It was Fredrica's old wooden wheelchair, used in her later years, after she had suffered a stroke. It had been kept as a prop after her death. But who had pushed it across the stage into that position? None of the students would admit to having done it as a joke. Besides, no one had been backstage where the chair had started its roll across the stage.

Others, including Burt Drexler, a former Iowa State speech professor, said that lights in the building would go on and off without reason.

Some said that Shattuck's ghost moved to the new Fisher Theatre in 1973 or1974. They believe that because of some strange things that have happened there.

One actor heard his name screamed out during a rehearsal. No one would take the blame.

When Joseph Kowalski, an assistant professor of theater, was looking for light switches in the dark upper backstage, a voice said, "They're over by the door." He found them, switched them on, but no one was up there with him.

At another time, Kowalski was working alone in the costume shop when, according to Ken Uy's article in the *Ames Daily Times* of

October 28, 1993, the items he was using, such as scissors and tape measure, disappeared. After a while, they appeared again—not where he would have left them as he worked, but all gathered together in one spot off to the side.

Another time, music came over the loudspeakers when no one had started it. When Brooks Chelsvig, the sound technician, arrived, he and Joe Libby, former house manager, went upstairs to look into it. The music stopped. When they unlocked the sound booth, they found one of Chelsvig's tapes in the tape deck. It had been played halfway through. But no one was there.

Kerry Bell, the co-house manager, and a friend went to Fisher the night before the opening night of *Rumors*. Kerry realized it was almost midnight, and her friend was dragging her feet about that, but they wanted to put up a display using the actors' photos. Riding the elevator back downstairs from the upper level, Kerry pushed the emergency stop button as a joke. She thought she might as well scare her friend a little. But as she switched it off again, the elevator still didn't move. Not until Kerry's friend screamed. Then the elevator moved back up to second floor and the doors opened. Needless to say, both Kerry and her friend left the building at a run.

All of these incidents seem to support the claims that the Shattuck ghost had moved to Fisher.

According to an article by Vicki Shannon in the *Iowa State Daily* of October 30, 1978, Molly Herrington explained the ghost this way: "She's just letting us know that she's still around. She comes out to tell us she's glad we're still doing theater at ISU, since she's the one who started it all."

Shannon quoted Herrington: "At night, ghosts will come out and re-enact their 'big scene.' Sometimes they put together a whole show." Herrington had also told Shannon that old theater troupes always left a gas lamp burning in the middle of the stage to show ghosts their way. Herrington believed in the Shattuck ghost of more recent times.

◁ 7 ▷

A Ghostly 'Coon-Hunting Story

Daniel J. Zoll had also joined us around the fire at Big Island, having spent the day fishing. He wanted to share a ghost story of his own. His parents used to operate a small country store a few miles north of Waukon in northeast Iowa called the Hanover Store. People would come by in the evening and sit around and talk and tell stories. One of the favorites was this one about 'coon hunting.

My father, Emmet Zoll, grew up in French Creek Township about seven miles north of Waukon, and used to tell this story: The October night it happened was dark, dark, dark. Low hanging, misty clouds obscured the stars and horizon. From the hilltop he could see little circles of light moving through the trees and brush below. It was the weekly gathering of the Silver Creek raccoon-hunting society finding their way through Gerkey's bottom land on Silver Creek. Each hunter carried a kerosene lantern that gave out a dim circle of yellow light, making progress through the deep grass, brush, and trees possible but an adventure, if not a bit hazardous.

The Silver Creek raccoon-hunting society was a loosely organized group dedicated to the hunting of the nocturnal masked bandit. Some declared that the group was more interested in finding John Barleycorn than raccoons, although that was vehemently denied by all participants. The members of the group, in the main, all grew up in Hanover and French Creek. Most were farmers, but a few had town jobs. The parish priests from Hanover and Lycurgas were honorary members and usually attended. Emmet was one of the charter members of the group.

Hunting was not very good this particular night. The dogs had treed only two raccoons. Toward midnight everyone was getting rather damp from the mist. Emmet suggested that he and his brother, Willie, should take a shortcut to the abandoned house at the upper end of the Gerkey farm and get a fire started so there would be a toasty meeting place for the usual social hour that followed every hunt regardless of its success.

They took Ol' Blue with them. Ol' Blue was the patriarch of the hound dogs. Going on thirteen years, he still had one of the best noses for raccoons around, but he couldn't keep up with the other dogs anymore.

When they reached the house, Willie got the firewood and Emmet started the fire in the old fireplace. While Emmet was doing that, he asked Willie to put Ol' Blue upstairs. The old house had been built in the 1880s and, like houses of that era, it had a very steep stairwell with a door at the bottom. Well, Willie helped Ol' Blue up the stairs, and the old dog wandered over next to the chimney and plopped down. Willie closed the door at the bottom of the stairwell so Ol' Blue could get some rest.

In about a half hour, the rest of the group dragged in and gathered around the fire to warm up and dry off. The fire by this time was burning brightly, casting flickering shadows around the room. Some of the group sat on the floor, but a few had pulled up some chunks of firewood and used them for a seat.

One of the Byrnes men was in charge of the refreshments for the evening. He went outside to his hiding place by a fencepost and came up with two jars of pure, homemade gut-warmer. As the men sat around the fire, sipping on the refreshments, the conversation soon got around to ghost stories and haunted houses, maybe because the hunting that night had been a complete bust. Apparently even the raccoons had the sense to stay home out of the damp and chill. In those days, people had strong beliefs about ghosts and hauntings. The stories got better and better as the fire burned down and the jars neared emptiness. Each storyteller tried his best to outdo the previous one.

At about this time, Bill Gerkey, whose grandfather had built the abandoned house they were in, asked, "Did you ever hear the story about the ghost who used to haunt this very house?"

Well, no one had, so Bill proceeded to tell the story about his grandfather's hired man who had lived upstairs in the house. He was a weird fellow who never said much, but he was a good worker. Well, a couple of nights before Halloween in the fall of 1886, Bill's grandfather heard the hired man wandering around upstairs. Suddenly, the man fell down the stairs. He broke his neck in the fall and died. Ever after, at the end of October, residents could hear someone upstairs. Bill added that his own grandparents always used to say that every year, around Halloween, they'd hear someone walking around upstairs, and then a loud crashing and banging down the stairway would follow.

The fire was dying down. There was a lull in the conversation while the last jar made its final pass around the room. It was then that Ol' Blue woke up and scratched himself a few times, his hind leg making a *thump, thump, thump* on the floor upstairs. Everyone in the room except Emmet and Willie froze. Then Ol' Blue got up, walked across the room, his nails going "click-clunk, click-clunk, click-clunk" across the ceiling just over their heads. Ol' Blue wasn't very good at navigating stairways, especially steep ones, and when he got to this one, he missed the top step and came *thump, bump, bang* down the stairs and with a loud thud, hit the door at the bottom.

Well, the rush to get out of that old house that miserable night was pretty impressive, especially considering just exactly how much moonshine had been passed around the group by the fire. The priest from Lycurgas led the charge, with the priest from Hanover right behind him. How so many people could get through a single doorway so fast in the dark is still a mystery to this day, but somehow they did. They made it back to their homes, too, without aid of their lanterns, which were still lined up on the porch. Emmet and Willie were splitting their guts with laughter when Ol' Blue licked Emmet's hand. He looked down and saw the old coonhound and realized he had come down unnoticed sometime during the story telling. Both Emmet and Willie stared at the dog, then swiveled their heads to the door at the bottom of the stairs. It was closed. They heard another *thump*.

In a minute, they were hightailling it out of the house, down the porch and into the inky black night right along with the rest of the hunters. They never did figure out how Ol' Blue had gotten downstairs.

◄ 8 ►

Let the Doctor Rest

After the wonderful story about the coon hunters, I remembered a story about my cousin Ernie and told that to the group around the campfire. Ernie lived in Grandview, Iowa, a small town of between three and four hundred in population, located east of Columbus Junction and not far from the Mississippi River running along the eastern border of the state.

Ernie rented a room during the week while working at a meat-processing plant in Columbus Junction. On weekends, he drove home to western Iowa to see his dad and spend time with him and with his family.

One of his co-workers at the plant told him about a doctor's house a short distance south of Grandview.

This co-worker had lived in the house some years before with his parents and siblings, and he considered the house to be haunted. His family reported that they felt an unseen presence on the stairs, sometimes passing family members. That, in itself, was upsetting, since there were children in the family who felt insecure on the stairs when they felt something passing but could see no one else there.

Another strange discovery was that windows which had been nailed shut were often found open later on, some opening when someone approached them.

All in all, people began to wonder what was happening in that house. But that co-worker's job changed. He and his family moved to another town, and Ernie lost contact with him. A succession of tenants occupied the house since then, no one staying very long.

The imposing two-story, red-brick house still makes quite an impression on those who pass by it to or from Grandview. Ernie said, "When I think of it now and then, I wonder if that former plant worker could tell me more about what happened when he lived in the doctor's house, but maybe I don't really want to know. If the doctor haunted it, I prefer to let him rest in peace."

◄ 9 ►

A Stroke of Luck

T hose Iowans were just full of stories that night around the fire at Big Island. Jillian, yet another of the Iowa residents to stop by, had a story of her own to share. She was a young reporter and had been given an assignment. She was to get a story at the Old Slave House, in Gallatin County, Illinois. She also had a personal mission. She wanted to prove that it was, after all, not haunted and just a big old house.

By late Saturday afternoon, Jillian had driven up to Gallatin County and found the place in question. While George, the current owner, conducted a tour, he informed Jillian that the John Crenshaw Hart family—who had built the house—called it Hickory Hill. John Crenshaw Hart had made a fortune mining natural salt springs in the valley. The young reporter could see that it was an especially well-built home, and its furnishings gave evidence of wealth. *But that was nearly 160 years ago*, she was thinking.

Jillian asked, "What is there about the house that draws so much attention now?"

George was on his guard immediately. He said, "You came here to get a story, Miss? You've seen the slave cabins and the iron kettles and the tunnels, and I've shown you all three floors of the house. Now you're on your own. You're welcome to investigate, any way you want to, just don't disturb the spirits here."

As the Old Slave House had room for travelers, Jillian asked, "Well, I figured I'd have to stay the night. Would you let me have the room Lincoln slept in once?"

George smiled but shook his head. "Nope. But I can give you the one directly above it." He winked.

"Great! I'm ready to go up there now. I'll get my things." The tour had taken more than an hour, and night had fallen. With the drive, Jillian admitted to being tired.

George escorted her to the room above The Lincoln Room.

Sitting on the handsome bed, Jillian finished her brown-bag sandwich while she made notes. *This is going to be a really dry story, as dry as this sandwich*, she thought as she put her notebook down and stretched out on the bed.

The ceiling light didn't make for very good reading, but she managed to read a couple stories from *Dixie Ghosts* to get her in the mood. The first one didn't shake her up much. The second one was just getting interesting when the book slid from her hands and her head nodded.

The sound that woke her was like a crack, as if pieces of wood were being hit together. It seemed to come from above, but it was muffled. She remembered George saying that the high ceilings were extra thick. Coming wider awake, she wondered who was up on third floor in the middle of the night. *But that's silly*, she thought. *All that's up there now is dried up evidence of what went on many, many years ago!*

Jillian thought of the whipping posts and the small cell-like rooms and bunks that George had shown her. She made a mental note to get some good photos in the morning. She remembered that Uncle Bob's room was the larger one with the sign. She had seen an old rocking chair in there, and a cot. *But it's so dark, I'll have to use the flash.* That thought reminded her to turn out the ceiling light. She got into bed now, ready for a decent sleep.

She yawned and was soon asleep again. Until she woke up to the sound of footsteps on the stairs. Not the main stairway to the second floor, though. Those were carpeted. *That's on the long, narrow wooden steps that lead up to the third floor*, she realized. *But why would anyone go up there in the night?*

While she thought about that, she heard the distant sound of whimpering women and crying babies. That cleared the cobwebs from her mind. There was no more sleeping now. What has happened? What's going on?

Jillian thought she heard footsteps above her. They sounded like bare feet on bare wooden floors. Then it was more like the closing of wooden doors, followed by a louder "Crack!" this time. *Is someone up there fooling around with those whipping posts? Or trying out the whips? What a horrible thought! Jillian, calm down before you go absolutely berserk,* she told herself.

Listening intently, she thought she heard the folding doors opening back against the dining room wall downstairs. That sound was accompanied by the stomping of horses' hooves and a creaking of wagon wheels turning and picking up speed outside. Impossible! The sounds faded as they seemed to move down the wooded hillside below her window.

Wow! This place is getting to me. I've got to settle this once and for all. Or go crazy before Monday morning. And now I don't hear anything at all. Is it over? Or did I just turn stone deaf? or . . . did everyone else leave?

She shivered in her pajamas. Grabbing her sweater from the foot of the bed, she slipped it on. It was late October, and she was further north than her home in Iowa. She wondered just how chilly it was outside. *It's sure cold in here all of a sudden. Oh, yeah—in that book, there was something about spine-chilling stories and cold spots where the ghosts enter and leave a room. Well, this could be a ghost story shaping up, but I've still got to get to the bottom of it! Only way to do that is to get up to the top floor.*

Some time before dawn, she dressed and tiptoed out into the hall and over to the narrow wooden stairs. She remembered noticing how worn they were when George took her up there the day before.

Climbing the steps carefully, Jillian hoped they wouldn't creak and wake the owner's family. *He said I was on my own, so he won't come with me anyway.*

She reached the top step. Crossing the wide hallway to one of the small rooms, she passed the whipping posts. They looked undisturbed.

With the help of her flashlight, she saw shackles hanging from a hook and chains heaped on the floor. She read the sign outside Uncle Bob's room. How horrible it must have been up here when Crenshaw was in the business of the illegal slave trade!

She wanted a closer look at that room, and maybe a photo. Her flashlight fell while she took her camera out. Aiming the lens toward the interior of the room, she took the chance that the photo would turn out. With some moonlight coming in the big window at the end of the hall, she could barely see the rocking chair. But one thing she could see was that it was rocking! And the covers on the cot had been piled on the floor in a heap.

Then the voices started, first as from a distance, almost like a gentle breeze. Then stronger, and it was like hearing hundreds of men, women, and children speaking out in protest and in pain and anger. A wind suddenly came out of nowhere and tossed the voices back and forth until they seemed to bounce off the walls and ceiling.

Jillian was thoroughly shaken now. The idea of a good story had fled her mind. Now, all she wanted to do was get out of that attic and out of that house. But as she held her hands out and groped for the wall where she knew the steps had to be, she felt a filmy substance in the air. It was like trying to beat down massive cobwebs in an old barn. They clung to her hands and face and clothes and she couldn't rid herself of them.

Finally finding the stairway, she had to feel her way by moving her hands along the wall so she wouldn't fall off the open side of the steep steps. The wall was ice cold on her palms.

She took the last steps in a leap. She raced back to the guest room and grabbed her things. She couldn't get down to the first floor fast enough. *Why . . . there's light on in the Lincoln Room! It looks like someone tall and dark is lounging in a chair and reading!* Jillian stared, terrified. She tore herself from staring at the figure and made a beeline for the main stairs. She hit the main floor, then the front door, at a run and fled into the night. She was thankful her car started on her second try.

On her way down the hill and back to Route 13, Jillian calmed down enough to think: So Lincoln slept there. That was before the Civil War and the Emancipation Proclamation. Maybe he hadn't slept well. Maybe he heard the sounds of suffering and pain coming from the attic. Did he take a walk before breakfast and talk to children in the yard, or workers down by the salt furnaces? Did he figure out that the sounds on third floor were the sounds of captive slaves, uncooperative slaves being whipped at the post, crying babies taken from their mothers' breasts, whimpering girls and women and men being hauled away, only to be sold back into slavery? *If Lincoln heard all the sounds I heard, it might have been enough to turn him from the idea that slavery was okay.* But this is 1990. Jillian knew she'd never be able to prove what she had seen and heard, even if the experience had nearly scared her to death. And she knew she would have to face the gang in the newsroom on Monday morning! *They'll never believe me.*

When the Halloween edition of the paper came out, Jillian's lead was: "Biographies and histories say that Lincoln grew up with slavery and didn't see it as morally wrong until he visited John Crenshaw's Hickory Hill property. The historic site, also known as the Old Slave House, is in Gallatin County, Illinois."

Her story continued, "Tourists who visit the house in the 1990s may think it strange that Lincoln once spent a night there, because Crenshaw was engaged in the slave trade in a free state. It is said that he also treated slaves like animals and tortured them on the third floor of his home.

"This reporter, after her recent experience at the Old Slave House, thinks it was a stroke of luck that Lincoln spent a night there. Good luck. Good for the slaves and for our nation. Lincoln's experience that night may have helped change his views on slavery."

The rest of the article detailed Jillian's scary experience that night, laying the blame on no one but the spirits lingering from the days when the Crenshaw mansion was the setting of almost unbelievable activity.

◄ 10 ►

The Haunted Castle

I was at Wild River State Park in eastern Minnesota, enjoying the lovely campground one late summer day. This park had a notice board, and I thought I'd put up a note about wanting to gather some ghost stories. I invited campers to stop in at my site. Well, that sure worked. People stopped in readily and brought some really weird tales.

This story of the haunted castle at 121 Park Street, Guthrie, Kentucky, was told to me by some Ohio residents who had visited it. The mansion stood in all its dignity on the corner of a lovely residential neighborhood, waiting. Waiting for what? Waiting to be sold and made into a bed and breakfast? Or an antique shop? Waiting for the dear ladies who were once lovingly redecorating it to return and finish their work? Waiting for the captain to return, or his daughters?

Whatever the reason, the elegant house stood empty and idle— at least as far as a realtor's description would indicate.

Perhaps the house is sold by now. But a few years ago, it was still listed with realtors. That might be surprising, considering the quality and beauty of the structure and the loving care it had been given over the years.

Some folks who know about the house say that an old sea captain from the British Isles left the sea for one reason or another. Perhaps it was connected somehow to tragedy, perhaps not. At any rate, they say he came without his wife, but he brought his two daughters with him. He traveled all the way to Kentucky from Boston, and when he arrived he bought a corner property in Guthrie, a small town, where the side-by-side lots he chose provided plenty of space for an impressive house and a roomy yard.

But, it seems the captain didn't really want to forget about his former life. He sent for two stone masons from the British Isles. They built the house for him in about 1898. The total cost was reported to be $9,000, a rather hefty sum in those days. So that he would feel at home, the retired seaman requested that they build it to look as much like a lighthouse on the British coast as possible. Some think it looks more like a castle with a lighthouse at one corner, but the captain was happy with the effect.

That three-story tower—somewhat, at least, like a lighthouse—has tall, curved-glass windows and a smaller, round porthole-like window high in the curved wall. The tower was built large enough to have ample space for furniture on each floor as the stairway spins on up to the tower's second and third floors. One could look through the front porch windows and see the lower floor where the captain's daughters spent many hours. There were once small tables, chests, colorful rugs, and curtains. There was a case of books near two soft, deep-cushioned chairs. The house was built for the comfort of the captain and his girls.

The exterior of the house remained in surprisingly good condition, considering its age. Built of stone masonry, it was also beautifully trimmed and decorated. The wood trim is detailed with patterns repeated all around the house above the porches and doors and on the widow's-walk-type upper porches. The top of the tower has a pattern of blocks like a lighthouse or a castle turret might have.

The woodwork inside is unique. One person who saw it said, "I have never seen the same woodwork in another house." Others say that it needs refinishing by now, and the whole house needs more work over and above all that has been done in maintenance through the years.

In fact, that's exactly what two women from thirty or forty miles away in Tennessee were doing—restoring some of the woodwork—when they disappeared. They had inherited the house, and they were not young, frivolous girls easily shaken from their purpose. They knew what they were about. When the property became theirs, they took over with plans aplenty. They tackled the major task of restoration and worked at it steadily. Several years into the project, so the story goes, the ladies were still busy fixing it up. They had refinished the beautiful mantles and brought some furnishings of their own to add to the library tables and old sea chests and mirrors that remained of the captain's belongings.

Whatever happened, the two suddenly quit. They left their lacquer brushes and their paint cans and furniture and just . . . took off.

Alice, who was then the coordinator for the Clarksville-Montgomery County Tourist Commission not far away, had been in the house. She stopped there when some tourists asked if they could see "the castle."

That day, Alice talked to the women as they worked. The new owners said they planned to restore the house entirely to its former condition. Then they would move in. Alice admired the hand-carved staircase that spiraled up inside the tower. And the next time she had permission to enter the house, she saw the open lacquer cans with the brushes still in them, stuck tight by then, the cans and lids resting on numerous dried lacquer rings on the hearths and mantles.

Alice questioned the man who worked at the service station across the street at the time. He said, "I don't know what happened. 'Bout a week or ten days after you saw it when those women were workin' there, they just plain left. I didn't hear nothin', didn't see nothin' that'd give 'em a reason to bail. But they must've heard or seen somethin' that gave 'em a pretty good scare, 'cause they got in their car 'n' left without a word to me or anyone else. They didn't even close their paint cans 'n' brushes 'n' turpentine 'n' stuff. I guess the stuff just sat there 'n' sat there 'til it all dried up. Brushes stuck in the cans 'n' ev'rything. Real waste really. Far's I know, they haven't been back."

When asked about transfers of ownership of the property, Alice was told that it passed down in the sea captain's family—only to his descendants. Every time a new descendant moved in, a death occurred within a year or a year and a half or so. A death in the family, and usually in the house. Then that family or couple would leave, and it would start over again. Anyway, that's the story. And the house had never passed out of the family.

Some changes have been made over the years. One fairly recent owner put shutters on the inside of the curved-glass window of the front-porch level of the round tower, to prevent curious folks from seeing into the house. But the shutters have been pushed aside. No one admits to having done that.

Another owner, long ago, added a brick kitchen to the back of the house. From it, there is access into the older part of the house.

Eaves, downspouts, the heating system—all are there, just showing the effects of time and neglect, but most folks believe they could be repaired and made functional again without too much trouble or expense. When the house had been built, only the highest quality fixtures and funishings had been used.

Even the purple iris near the front porch steps and the lily-of-the-valley at the side of the house suggest that someone once cared for it and loved it as a home. Or do they indicate that someone who loved it tenderly still tends it? Was the captain's wife lonesome for her family? Did she find their new home in a new land and hover about to enjoy life a little longer than was scheduled for her? Did she stick around to see that her two lovely young daughters turned into respectable young ladies, with a little help from her?

What were the captain's motives in traveling so far from his previous home and the sea to establish a new home in a foreign land? Just who could have appeared again in later years to frighten the new owners out of their seemingly strong intentions to make the castle their home? Could it have been the old sea captain? A faithful member of his crew? His wife? Was she up in the attic looking for the leaks in the roof, so their efforts at refinishing the woodwork would be worth their while?

And why do the citizens of Guthrie who walk or jog down Park Street choose to cross the street before they get near that particular corner property? The better to see the total effect from a greater distance? Or perhaps to keep their distance from those many windows that permit a mysterious stranger to look down on them and wonder why they are looking up?

◄ 11 ►

Deep Down Scars

Sally, another visitor at Wild River, told us about her experiences. She thought she had found a pretty good place to live, one near Austin Peavy State University and her work at the Grill. It seemed like a nice quiet country home, where she could come to study and sleep.

Her find was a big, old red brick house just across the state line from a Clarksville, Tennessee, campground. In fact, if one drove out of the campground and took a left at the first corner, one would be across the state line, in Kentucky and almost on Sally's porch.

The place had been a farmstead, but someone else had bought the land around her place, so just the old house was left. This was something she could afford and handle. And after she finished college and got a job in Clarksville, she'd be near enough to keep on living there.

Sally knew she'd have no trouble directing anyone to her house. It was the only one for quite a stretch on that road. "First," she told us around the fire, "there's a church on the left. Then there's the state line marker on a post. The first house after that is mine. Everything else around there is farmland."

Folks said maybe the people who built the house back in the 1830s wanted it that way—no one else around —nothing but fields.

Someone had also told Sally that the house was once owned by the parents of a well-known writer. She wondered if the writer had enjoyed the privacy. Sally answered, "I could see it as maybe a place to concentrate, like I'll have to concentrate on my studies if I'm going to make it through college and work, too."

36

Sally especially liked the ballroom above the dining room, in the new wing added in 1860. She wondered if the owner who added that wing was a wealthy southern gentleman who patterned the ballroom and the wide staircase after the plantations of the South. Sally pictured ballroom scenes she had loved in Margaret Mitchell's *Gone With the Wind* and in the movie version she watched over and over.

She could see the house decorated in holiday seasons for family and friends to meet in joyful celebration. She could even picture it during sad occasions. *Great things must have taken place in this house in past years, compared with the quiet life I plan to live here,* she thought.

As Sally settled in, she told us she got used to being in the house alone and welcomed the quiet hours. There was a lot going on, on campus, where there were people everywhere. It was hard to find a really quiet corner, even for those brief times she found to do the assigned readings for Advanced Modern Literature. At the Grill, there was never a dull moment. She was on her feet every minute, and glad to get off them and drive home. It was often between eleven and twelve before she pulled into the old carriage drive and used her special key to open the back door.

She'd had the security system built in simply because she would often be alone out there and didn't relish the idea of meeting up with strangers. Now, as she walked through the big kitchen to drop her book bag onto the dining room table, she was glad she could close the door and feel safe.

In a matter of weeks, though, things started happening, she told us, her eyes widening. Everyone seemed to lean closer to her. One day she was raking leaves when she thought she saw someone cross the drive between the back door and the empty carriage house.

Must have been a shadow, she told herself.

The next morning she woke up hearing things. It sounded like someone was playing fiddle music, and someone was dancing, maybe waltzing, up in the ballroom. She listened harder. Yes—one, two, three; one, two three in perfect waltz rhythm! *Am I imagining things? Is the quiet getting to me, or what?*

Then there was Saturday morning, when she heard a noise in the dining room and went to check it out. Her books were on the floor, with pages from her neatly organized folders mixed up and scattered all over the room.

That day, the neighbor-farmer, Fred, was out on the driveway hitching a trailer to his pickup. She ran out to catch him before he drove off.

"Hi, there, Sally! How's it going today?"

"Not great. Did you see anyone nosing around the house lately?"

"When? Just now?"

"No, the day I was out here raking leaves. I thought I saw someone back by the carriage drive."

"Wasn't me. I was out in the field. And I didn't see anyone else when I came in."

Sally told Fred about the books and about the dancing upstairs and the shadow.

"Well," he said, "let's go have a look." He climbed down from his big John Deere and preceded her into the house.

But, search as they might, there was no evidence of anyone having entered the house uninvited.

"Maybe we should look up in the ballroom, too." Sally asked, "Can you take the time?"

"Yah, I got time. Just have to make it to town by noon."

They found nothing up in the ballroom except an accumulation of dust on the worn floor. No footprints, no musicians, no dancers.

"Nothin' here. Did anyone tell you about the basement?"

Sally blinked and felt a tightness in her belly. "What about the basement? I haven't been down there since the realtor hurried me through it. Haven't had the water heater checked yet, or anything."

"Well, then, let's go have a look, and I'll tell you what I heard."

Whatever the mood of the ballroom had been, the basement suggested an entirely different atmosphere.

Fred said, "They say they used to hold runaway slaves here until they could return them to their masters. The original family was kind to their slaves, but some others weren't, and some of the mistreated slaves tried making their way to freedom in the north. If they were caught, they were sometimes sent here and held temporarily down here by chains."

Sally was beginning to wonder what else Fred knew.

"See," he said, "up here on this sturdy rafter is where the arm chains were fastened. See those huge bent nails? The leg shackles must've been fastened to those upright supports. You can see where they were secured. After the first owners sold the house in the 1870s and moved away, the slave chains were discovered."

"No wonder the realtor rushed me through this part of the house!"

"It could be that several owners passed the property onto new buyers by the time anyone spoke of the chains openly. Folks didn't like to talk about such things, even after the war. But a young couple who rented the house later on said someone had removed the chains before they moved in. Or maybe took them for souvenirs."

Sally thought, Or maybe they just never really found them. As she shivered at the thought, she decided that the scars and the suffering felt in that basement must have lived on, long after the chains were used. Lived on in the spirit, if not in the flesh. Just thinking about it gave her goose bumps.

Well, Sally had a choice. She could keep her big, old house with its quiet location in the middle of farmland and near work and school, or she could sell and hope to find someplace as comfortable and convenient. She looked around. Finally, she decided the old house was the perfect house for her and she really didn't want to move. But how to accommodate the spirits living there?

She had a basement bulkhead door installed in the back of the house, but, instead of putting a padlock on the outside as most people tended to do, she had one installed on the inside with the key hung on a hook right next to it. That way, should any lingering spirit want out, it only had to open the bulkhead and leave.

In the weeks following this, she found the bulkhead open seven times. When this happened, she would simply go down into that dark basement, close the bulkhead and lock it up again, making a show of putting the key back on the hook. After that, the music in the ballroom stopped, things around the house remained quietly in their place or where she had left them, and the bulkhead remained locked, and Sally enjoyed her peace and quiet in the old house just across the state line from Clarksville, Tennessee.

⟨ 12 ⟩

Cracked Mirrors, Death Signs

Gladys, a friend of Sally, had also come up to camp on Wild River and insisted on telling us a story of her own. A number of years ago, she told us around the campfire, she was spending the day in her comfortable home in Clarksville, Tennessee.

After she finished the chores around the house, she ran errands to the grocery store and post office, paid her utility bills, and returned a book to the Clarksville Library. She set up a time to have her car serviced, and then went home for lunch.

After lunch, Gladys stretched out on the davenport just to get off her feet a bit. She thought, *I have a whole hour before I have to leave for the museum.* She was one of the many volunteers who helped out with tours at the Clarksville-Montgomery County Historical Museum.

She lay thinking about some of the artifacts in the museum and how often she had led the tours that were becoming routine for her. It was quiet in the house, and she soon fell asleep . . . until a sound woke her.

It was a tiny sound. To her it seemed like the sound of a piece of pecan shell falling to the floor when someone hurriedly picked out the pecan meats for baking. Or it might have been the sound of a paper clip or an earring falling a few feet. That first sound was followed by a louder one, a sort of scraping, grating sound, something like when someone scratches on a window with a tough thumbnail or a nut pick.

Fully awake by then, Gladys looked toward the windows. Nothing there. She looked around the room. Everything looked all right. But then she noticed that a new wall mirror across the room looked different. When she got up to look more closely, she saw that it had started to crack, but in a strange way. Not from the edge as if it had been rudely bumped against a wall or at a corner as if it had been dropped, but more from the center. As she watched, the crack continued to grow, coming around to form a little circle in the middle. A chill shook her.

"Well!" Gladys said out loud to the mirror. "You go back to the store tomorrow! I'll have to get a replacement for you before the kids come home. They'd better give me a good deal at the store, too. I thought I had bought a perfect mirror!"

As she settled back on the davenport, she thought, *That'll be nice, having the family home for a while. Not quiet, but . . .* and she dozed off once more.

But she was soon awake again. That same small sound. She got up and looked at the wall mirror, but it had not changed. The sound drew her to the framed coat rack mirror over by the front door, and, again, she watched as a perfect circle cracked in the middle of the mirror. She knew something wasn't right.

What did cracked mirrors mean? Two of them cracking in the same strange way on the same day with no apparent cause. *That wouldn't just happen,* she thought as she lifted them both down from the wall.

How was the circle significant was one question in her thoughts as she drove to the museum. She knew the symbolism of a circle. Was the crack in the mirror signaling the end of a life? The breaking off of a relationship? Maybe within the family?

These were not the first death signs to come to her, and, when they appeared, they always proved out. Like this time. Before night, a phone call informed Gladys that her Aunt Jeannie had been in a bad accident involving her car and a semi. Aunt Jeannie was pronounced dead at the scene.

Gladys had come to accept unexplainable occurrences like doors closing upstairs when she was downstairs, or footsteps on the stairs when she was alone in the house. Or the doorbell ringing in the night when no one was there ringing it. She sort of tossed these things off and mostly laughed at them.

Sometimes photos fell off the walls. Not family photos. Just scenic art. Her son Michael had a hobby of photographing interesting or colorful scenes in state and national parks and monuments and having enlargements made. The result was that she had a number of framed color photos of nature scenes decorating her walls. When one of them fell to the floor, she told herself the nails were just too small, or there wasn't a stud behind the plaster to hold the nails. Her theory was that when they fell, it wasn't because anything bad had happened, just something wrong with the technology of hanging the pictures.

But the more she thought about it, the more she believed that the present unusual activity had something to do with the family, none of whom lived nearby. Would the next photo that fell be one of a relative? One of her children? Would it be a death sign?

One thing more. When her family arrived the next day, they heard about the mirrors. In fact, they saw them leaning against the wall as soon as they came into the house.

Mike teasingly asked, "What did you do, Mom, go on a breaking spree?" Daughter-in-law Donna's question was, "How could two mirrors break in the exact same way, and one of them the brand new one?"

That brought Gladys to tell them all of what had been happening—not only the mirrors, but the sounds and the photos falling and the earlier incidents that she felt were death signs.

Donna said, "No wonder the girls had a funny feeling sometimes when we were here visiting you. We didn't want to tell you before. But they never felt comfortable or could sleep soundly in that northwest room upstairs. It was always as if someone else was there, too. And it was always kind of cold in there, at least off and on."

"Well, then," Gladys said, "maybe we do have a visitor—an extra one—one that hovers here like a spirit, in touch with distant family and with a desire to bring them closer somehow, or something like that."

The end result was that Gladys switched the furnishings of a couple of upstairs rooms. She made the northwest bedroom into her sewing room so as not to upset her grandchildren anymore. And maybe—just maybe—she would have company there herself, as she sat at the sewing machine to do the mending.

‹ 13 ›

But, Where Is Eric?

But Gladys wasn't done yet. She had another ghost story to tell, this one about the Bell Witch Cave near Adams, Tennessee, an ideal place, her daughter thought, for a seance. Gladys admitted that life was probably pretty boring for the Clarksville teenagers, and boredom was probably the reason that led her daughter, Paula, and her friends to the cave one late October day.

After waiting a while for one of their number to arrive, they decided to walk down to the cave entrance. Paula said, "Let's hope Eric makes it before dark." Eric had to work. "I hope he doesn't have to stay too late!" Eric was the one who knew more about the caves and had done all the research on the witch, whom he called Crazy Kate.

Paula and her friends were already into a seance when they heard Eric's motorcycle screech to a stop above the wooded bank of the Red River. After the motor cut out, however, they heard nothing. Concentrating hard on calling spirits, the group in the cave didn't call out to Eric. *He knows we're here*, Paula thought. *He'll have seen my Pinto.*

Then Paula forgot about Eric altogether as she concentrated on calling spirits. A sweet singing suddenly filled the cave, and Paula felt prickles crawl up her arms. The song came gradually louder and clearer until it bounced from the walls and echoed in the enclosure.

Eric's trying to scare us, thought Paula, although the voice singing sounded female.

The music increased in volume until the very rocks of the cave floor seemed to be vibrating with the notes, tossing the melody back and forth and up to the walls and ceiling until it all got mixed up and and run together as if a group of voices sang a round.

> *The ears of the cave witch*
> *how clearly they hear you*
> *a-cursing and shouting*
> *and calling her name.*
> *The ears of the Bell witch*
> *they hear you a-calling*
> *and if you don't leave*
> *you'll be sorry you came.*
> *I'll get you . . . I'll kill you . . .*

Paula felt her heart begin to race. Had Eric brought others to sing with him? What was he doing? But she didn't ponder long. Pandemonium broke loose. The song changed to shouts, raucous threats, and curses. Then other sounds began, like rumblings from deep back in the second room or from the overhead passage. And the winds picked up—powerful crosscurrents that lashed at Paula and her friends, whipping at them until they pulled each other up and stumbled out of the cave. Once outside, the noises instantly ceased and the wind fell away. They walked out into the perfect calm of a tranquil evening.

Out of breath and wild-eyed from the experience, it took them a while to adjust to the difference. Evening had followed dusk. The stars were out, and the moon wore a big, tilted smile. There was a hint of late October chill in the air.

Then the friends came to their senses and scrambled up the root-bound slope toward their cars. Eric's Harley was parked next to the cars. But . . . where was Eric? No one ever saw him again.

⊰ 14 ⊱

Kate Walks at Midnight

Virgil Barnes cleared his throat, and I jumped, dropping the stick I was about to add to the campfire. Other people around the fire exclaimed. The story about Eric had spooked us. Virgil chuckled. He was a man in his early nineties, white haired (what was left, that is) and wrinkled, his face looking like weathered leather. He wanted to tell us another Bell witch story.

Virgil had done his courting in the horse and buggy days, he said. One night when he was seventeen or eighteen, he was heading home. The horse knew the way, so he loosened the reins and dozed, letting old Ben take him and the buggy home. He had just left his sweetheart sitting on her parents' porch swing, so Virgil was alone.

It was almost midnight when his horse led him past the area where the old Bell home place was, about nineteen miles from Clarksville, Tennessee, and forty-three miles from Nashville. Virgil wasn't paying much attention. Suddenly his horse shied. Jerked in the buggy, Virgil looked up just in time to see a woman, head down, in a flowing white dress, walking slowly down the side of the road.

The horse snorted loudly and sidestepped again. Then with a whinny, it spooked and took off, pell mell.

With the buggy bouncing along behind the galloping horse, it took a few minutes for Virgil to get his hands on the reins again and haul back. When the horse finally slowed down and Virgil had time to think, he wondered who the woman had been. He hadn't recognize her, for sure, and he knew most everyone in the area. He hadn't been able to see her face. "And that's what makes it so strange," he said to his father the next morning, as he told him what had happened.

Virgil's father agreed. "It is strange. Womenfolk don't go out at night these days, here in the country. And even if they did, they'd speak or wave or . . . something."

"That's why I was so bafffled. She didn't even look up to greet me. Then old Ben went nuts and took off. So, I didn't get a chance to speak, either. Matter of fact, I didn't know what to make of it! And it all happened so fast!"

The story spread widely in the close community, but no one knew who that woman was. No one ever stepped forward and said she had been walking on that road that night.

"I'm convinced it was the Bell witch," Virgil told our group around the fire. "Old Ben was as calm an old farm horse as ever there was. Nothing flapped him usually, but he would never let me or anyone else drive him down that road after that night. Not even in the bright sun of day. He'd rear and neigh and pretty much dig his heels in and refuse to move. Sweat would break out all over him until he looked as lathered as if he'd just run the Kentucky Derby."

Life went on for Virgil Barnes in spite of that strange incident. At nineteen, he married—not to that particular sweetheart he had seen that night—but to Lovie Pitt, a neighbor girl. They lived in peace, in the same area, across the Red River from the old Bell farm and the Bell Witch Cave near Adams, Tennessee. Lovie lived into her eighties.

Virgil's closing comment was, "I don't know who she was, and I probably never will. I don't care to know. Maybe she was the Bell witch the folks around here call Kate. Whoever she was, or whatever, I only know I never want to see her again!"

⊰ 15 ⊱

Kate Haunts the Antique Mall

We weren't done with the Bell witch yet. Nina, who also hailed from the area, had her own story to tell. After she had let her dogs in from the playground, Nina locked the side door of the complex that included the antique store she managed. No one else was there, so she let the dogs chase each other around the hall for a while, but only for a short while. Too often, they knocked something down and broke it before she sent them down to the basement for the night.

"I liked having those two big dogs," she told us. "They made me feel safer. Bouncer and Thrasher were only mixed breeds, but they were big. They had some St. Bernard in them, maybe, or something else big and hairy. But they were very gentle. They never barked during the day, but if someone came around at night, they'd let loose with deep, rumbly barks and growls, but they'd never bite anyone. During the day, they'd just lie around the basement like beached whales, ignoring people as they came in and walked around above them. And 'my boys' were good company for me when there weren't any tourists around. They were my security system and my buddies."

Nina recalled a Saturday night when Bouncer and Thrasher started barking in the middle of "Opry House" entertainment up on the second floor. When she went down to check on them, the dogs acted funny, wary almost, but she couldn't see why. This was very unusual behavior for them.

Another time just a month later, when the shop had opened for the day and a few browsers were moving from room to room, the dogs barked furiously and scratched on the basement door, pawing at it as if they wanted out of the old boiler room now. When Nina finished packing and wrapping a washbowl and pitcher set someone from Minnesota had bought, she went to see why the dogs were acting up. Everything but the dogs seemed fine. Nothing was there, even though the dogs acted agitated. Maybe it was just a mouse, Nina thought. Or a snake. Snakes were always getting into that basement.

Antiques and collectibles filled all the rooms of the first floor of the building that had once been classrooms. Some cabinets and shelves filled the halls, too. It was all pretty crowded. Nina had books, too. On a table in the entrance, there were stacks of books about the area. One was a black-covered paperback, *The Bell Witch of Tennessee*, by Charles Bailey Bell, a descendant of John Bell. Another was titled *Echoes of the Bell Witch in the Twentieth Century*. Those books were about the Bell family, especially those members plagued the most by the Bell witch.

From her position at the cash register, Nina could see when people were interested in the books. She liked to tell them, "If you buy a book about her and leave it somewhere, the witch'll cause it to disappear." This was one of the things told about the witch. Tourists either got scared and put the book down or became curious and bought it to see if that really happened.

Nina called her shop "The Bell Witch Village Antique Mall," and her black and white business card used a witch figure next to the printed information. The shop was at Adams, Tennessee, ten miles north of Springfield on Highway 41 and forty miles from Nashville.

The old brick Bell School, originally built on the Bell family property, made as good an antique mall as any. People could wander into any room there, but they always came back by the cash register counter before they left by the double front doors, the logical way to get back to the parking lot. This brought Nina quite a bit of business.

On Saturday nights, the school's old auditorium on the second floor was put to use for entertainment. The rows of folding seats and the stage are still there, and the whole is referred to as the Opry House. Community performers entertain locals and tourists every Saturday night.

Nina visited with many of the people who came through. Ann and Carrie, for example. They were sisters back visiting their "old school." They said they had attended grade school in the building. They knew some pretty strange happenings and stories from the school's early days.

One story was that a man from North Carolina brought slaves with him. The slaves' master was angry and pushed a slave into a vat of lye soap, scalding him to death. "Or so the story goes," Carrie said, "that's the way I heard it."

Another was that the Bell daughter Betsy and her fiancé Joshua Gardner never married because the witch had threatened that, should a Bell ever married a Gardner, she would come back and haunt them.

Ann said the witch, sometimes called Kate, tormented people. She seemed to have a deep hatred for John Bell, causing him much physical and mental discomfort. After his death, folks said Kate came in the night and switched a bottle of poison for his medicine.

They said that Kate could speak sweetly to John's wife, Lucy, but used foul language while speaking to others. She seemed to have a tender spot for Lucy. When Lucy was very sick, Kate appeared and dropped luscious bunches of grapes and nuts from a foreign land into her lap to help her recover.

Carrie said that when the witch was tormenting someone, folks would hear her slapping their cheeks, and they saw the cheeks, often Betsy's, turn red. And when the Bell family had guests, the witch vowed there'd be no sleep in that house. Then she proceeded to pull the covers off the Bell children and the visitors in the middle of the night.

But the women said the witch was gone long ago. They had even heard why. The story was that if someone shot the witch or her shadow with a silver bullet, she'd go away. One brave soul got as far as rolling a silver bullet to use on the shadow he assumed was the witch, but before he had the bullet ready, the shadow disappeared and never came back.

When Nina was questioned about the witch, she vowed that strange things went on there at the old school, even yet. One thing she couldn't explain was that one night when the Opry House was emptied after the Saturday night performance, and the audience and entertainers had left the building, the dogs started acting up again. She listened, and she heard a loud clapping up in the auditorium. She took the two big dogs up with her to check, but not a soul was there. At least, not any she could see.

Other times, she felt as though something light in substance passed her on the stairs or in the halls. Even in the old classrooms, she sometimes heard voices and turned, expecting to answer a visitor's question, only to find no one there.

Since the books Nina had in the front of the store did not disappear (though once she thought so but later found them buried in a different pile), and since Carrie and Ann said the witch had never appeared after the silver bullet was made ready, no direct harm evern came to Nina or to tourists who stopped by to satisfy their curiosity.

Nina said, "I still keep Bouncer and Thrasher close by and lock that side door after I let them in at night." But then she laughed. "As if a locked door would ever stop a witch."

◄ 16 ►

A Child's Voice Cried, "Mom-m-m-y-y!"

Nancy and Ken, up from North Carolina, were vacationing in Minnesota as part of a cross-country tour in their motor home. She saw the crowd around my campfire and joined us in time to hear a couple of the Bell witch stories. In the lull that followed Nina's story, she spoke up to tell us about some spooky happenings they had heard about in their travels. She prefaced her story with a bit of history.

"General James Winchester, a hero in the Revolutionary War, came from Maryland to Tennessee in 1785. He and his brother George took land grants for their service in the war. They chose a beautiful part of middle Tennessee with native forest, buffalo trails, and perils from hostile Indians. Most of this history is in *Long, Long Ago*, by Susan Black Winchester Scales. It's a collection of reminiscenses of Cragfont. As things turned out, George Winchester was killed by Indians, but Cragfont, built on the site the two had chosen along Bledsoe's Creek, became the home of General James Winchester and his bride, Susan Black Winchester, as well as their fourteen children. The home remained in the family until 1864."

Nancy and Ken took a tour through Cragfont. Also at that campground, the guide, Kim, told us about the house and the Winchester family who built it and occupied it for many years.

General Winchester chose Cragfont as the name of his home (started in 1798 and finished in 1802) because it stood on a rocky bluff (a crag) at the base of which was a spring (a font).

"But my purpose here is not to describe Cragfont in detail, nor to tell the story of life as it was for all the Winchesters," Nancy said. "I want to tell about the strange happenings there through the years as well as our experience as we visited there, just before we went on our way."

Kim and her husband, caretakers when Nancy and Ken were there, lived in the log house behind the mansion. Kim got our interest as she said, "In the big house, we've heard the flutter of petticoats, the patter of little feet on the steps to the nursery, and heavier footsteps behind us as we ascend or descend those stairs."

She told Nancy and Ken of other strange occurrences as she led them through the house. She may have mentioned more of them than usual. Some visitors would have felt uncomfortable if told about those happenings while right inside the house. But Ken had told Kim that Nancy wrote ghost stories for publication, so she filled them in thoroughly on what went on. Nancy, of course, took notes.

"In the plantation office," Kim said, "a rifle is hung horizontally above the mantle. Often, when none of us conducting tours or doing housekeeping has moved it, we'll find the rifle off the wall and propped against a chair. That happens day or night," Kim said.

"Sometimes," she continued, "this open case displaying General James Winchester's cockade hat and epaulets will be closed, or the daybook nearby in the same room will be found opened. We talk about this happening, but someone always says, 'Maybe it was one of the group you were taking through on a tour. Maybe they handled it or moved it, and you didn't notice.'" Kim wasn't so sure.

Nancy and Ken were shown the two large portraits in heavy frames that usually hung on the front foyer walls. Kim said, "In the morning, when we open the house, we sometimes find those portraits on the floor, face up, undamaged. But the portrait of Mrs. James Winchester above the mantle in the sitting room is never disturbed."

She showed us that if we stood at the inner end of the front foyer, between there and the hallway, and looked up the stairway, the doors of the secretary in the upper hallway were in view. She said, "Those doors will sometimes be open. We like them closed, and they were probably left closed the last time anyone went by it. Anyone human, that is."

Kim showed us a book titled *History of England* by Thomas Barrington Macaulay. Its old spine was cracked from the book being opened so many times. She said that General Winchester's father came from England. "We usually keep that book on a shelf in the secretary here," she said. "But quite often, we find it laid open on the writing board of the secretary, and it's always open to the same page that refers to that part of England. And I used to put Mrs. Winchester's cross in that book, but it was always taken out and laid in plain view. None of us who work in the house could figure out why, when, or how these things were changed. Now, I put the cross in a drawer, and it isn't disturbed any more."

Nancy and Ken followed Kim as she led them to a bedroom. "In the master bedroom, an original framed mirror is sometimes taken off the wall and propped against the chest. We also sometimes find the writing chair turned toward the window, as if a writer was more comfortable or more easily inspired while gazing out of doors instead of looking toward the furnishings of the room."

By then, Nancy and Ken were in the middle of the master bedroom, looking toward the bed. Kim said, "Another really scary thing happens here. It's a good thing you're used to writing and thinking about ghosts because this easily spooks most people. One impression, but often two, will be found on the bedcovers as if one or two persons had lain on the bed. The 'dents' where their heads would lie on the pillows are visible, too. We even measured once, and the bodies would have to be four-foot-ten and five-foot-seven. We do a careful check before we close the house each evening and lock it, and it still happens, even though there's no one in the house."

As we went down the upstairs hall, Kim said, "Heavy breathing is sometimes heard in the house, outside near it, or on the phone, even in our cabin, and my husband and I and others hear doors opening and closing and the sounds of something very heavy being dragged up or down the stairs here in the big house.

"The people responsible for the house keep regular hours for tours. Once a woman came to tour the house when it wasn't open. She returned later for a tour, but she had an unusual comment to make when she saw the portrait on the wall in the sitting room. She said, 'Why, there's the woman I saw in the window earlier when I couldn't get in. I looked up from the yard just before we drove away, and that lady was standing at this upstairs window.'"

As Nancy and Ken followed Kim up the stairs to the third floor, Kim told them that the Winchester children were sent up there when adult parties were held in the house. There was even a bed in case one of the children was not well. Apparently something happened up there because unexplainable sounds, such as the patter of feet going up the steps, sometimes hurriedly, is often heard. Some people have seen the figure of a blonde girl of five or six next to and below a window, in a corner up on that floor.

While we were on third floor, Kim told the couple, "Some of our workers have heard her crying and calling out 'Mommy! Mommy!' And sometimes a patch of light will show up in that room, on the painted brick wall above the fireplace. People who spend a lot of time here helping with tours during the busy season have talked to that light, and they say it blinks to answer them, though I've never seen it happen.

"We've tried placing a tape recorder in a couple of locations here. Once, on the tape, when someone asked, 'Are you angry?' a male voice answered 'No.' Several nights, we left a tape recorder near the stairway to third floor. It recorded sounds of something being dragged up and down the stairs. At various times, people have gone through the house carrying pocket-type tape recorders. Though they had heard nothing, when they played the tape back, they heard the cries of a child, followed by an adult voice some distance away calling out, 'Sita' or 'Sweethaht' or maybe even 'Cynty.' It's hard to distinguish the name exactly. We wonder if a little girl named Cynthia or Cynta or something similar died here."

About then, Ken and Nancy looked at each other as if questioning the validity of Kim's tales. But she was telling us more. "We've heard windows banging on third floor, where the windows are smaller than below and they're framed so that there could be no motion from the wind. And we've heard banging on our own headboard in the house provided for us out back in the yard."

After their tour, Nancy and Ken looked around in the flower garden and saw a few familiar flowering plants and herbs. It was the middle of April, so the bleeding heart and jonquils had finished blooming, but the pansies and Sweet Williams were colorful. They sat in the gazebo for a few minutes before stepping over the rock wall into the family cemetery far enough to see that there were several above-ground as well as numerous in-ground burial sites. The readable tombstones recorded deaths from long ago.

"We realized it was time to move on if we were to reach our camping site in nearby Hendersonville by dark," Nancy told her audience around the Minnesota campfire. "As we started toward our vehicle, we hesitated. Both of us had heard something that caught our attention. Was someone crying? Was that a child's voice? We paused at the rock wall, to listen. We were sure we were hearing a child crying, but it seemed to originate from beyond the rock wall and far, far down the rocky bluff where the stone for Cragfont's sturdy walls had been quarried so long ago. What we heard had sounded like a child, either hurt or very, very lonely, crying out, "Mom-m-m-y-y!" in a prolonged wail. We were just about to go back to the house to tell Kim that a child was lost and crying down there somewhere. But then, just as surely as we had heard it, we could hear it no longer. Then Kim's stories came to mind and we looked at each other. Ken's eyes were wide, and I bet mine were too. At that moment, we were absolutely sure what we were hearing, and, let me tell you, it creeped us out. We hurried on our way, but we are still wondering."

◄ 17 ►

Knob-and-Spool Wiring, Braces and Bits

I had traveled to a small KOA near Clearwater, Minnesota. Not a large campground, it did feature a nice swimming pool and a convenience store as well as a really nice county park just down the road where one could swim and hike—Warner Lake County Park. The really nice feature of this particular campground, however, one that lent itself to the telling of ghost stories, was that a graveyard bordered the KOA. Lots of inspiration there!

Lloyd, visiting Minnesota in his camper from Savannah, Georgia, joined a large group of us as we leaned against the fence with the graveyard behind us and told stories. He said that William J. Kehoe had been interviewed a few years earlier for a feature in the *Savannah News Press*. From the middle of five generations of William J. Kehoes, he said one could build several stories around the contributions and endeavors of those Kehoes, but what was relevant to Lloyd's story was that William's grandfather built the old family home at 123 Habersham Street in Savannah in 1893.

Almost a century later, the former Kehoe mansion was to be used for the 1981 Designer Showcase, "an interior decorators' display sponsored as a benefit by the Historic Savannah Foundation, Inc.," according to Ann Marshall Daniels, the staff writer who did the interview.

About twenty designers had signed up for space in the huge, old house. Each planned to make his or her space beautiful, though no one would be living in it except "imaginary inhabitants." The public would pay to take a look.

That's how it happened that Lloyd was up on the fourth floor with his stepladder and various tools. Lloyd had been hired by a contractor to do some preliminary work in the house before the designers had their go.

It was autumn of 1981, nearing the end of October. Lloyd's job was to check the electrical wiring throughout the house and replace it, if necessary, to make the house safe for the Designer Showcase. That meant he had to check the basement and all four floors above it. He had already worked his way up to the fourth floor. From the looks of the brittle, frayed wiring, he had decided this was either the original wiring or had been installed in an early renovation many years before. He had to remove the old knob-and-spool system and replace it practically everywhere.

As he worked at his customarily slow but steady pace, Lloyd thought about the house and the Kehoes for whom it had been the family home. This, he realized, would be a big change from the way the first William J. Kehoe had built the house before the turn of the century. Lloyd knew that the "transplanted Irishman" had chosen a small lot, then filled it with this tall, red-brick house. He had added balconies, railings of ironwork, and a cupola at the very top. With windows on all sides of the cupola, William could see north to the Savannah River and east to his red-brick ironworks at the end of Broughton Street. Among other items—such as sugar pans, sugar mills, and sewer covers, the cast iron railings were a specialty of the Kehoe Iron Works. They were not only durable, but also a remnant of the past that could still easily be found in use in the older parts of the city. They were fast becoming treasured antiques.

Habersham, a long street running through downtown Savannah, was interrupted by Whitefield Square, Troup Square, Columbia Square, and Warren Square. Near the riverfront was Emmett Park. Beyond it came riverfront plazas and streets with shops, museums, bike trails, and parking areas.

The 1893 Kehoe House was not far from the one at 130 Habersham, just across Columbia Square. The old family home was very familiar to the middle William J. Kehoe, who, as a boy growing up, was often in the home his grandfather built.

When William, now elderly, stepped into his grandfather's old family home in 1981, he was surprized by how steep the steps seemed and how many bedrooms there were. He had forgotten some details over the years, and the steep stairs left him short of breath. But he remembered how large the family was. "At mealtimes," he said, "the children had to eat in a second shift because the older family members easily filled all the places at the dining room table."

He also recalled the cupola his Uncle Jimmy had at the top of the house. Though it had been removed in a later renovation and a railing had been placed around the flat space, he knew the cupola had its advantages. With windows on all sides, not only was there a perfect view of the city in all directions, but the room also enjoyed breezes even on hot summer nights.

Lloyd said that there were numerous tales told in Savannah about the Kehoe House. One was that the original, fancy furnishings were scattered during the 1920s, replaced by furnishings with plainer shapes and straighter lines. Later, even those furnishings disappeared. It was said, too, that the house was once a funeral home.

Lloyd didn't spend much time on tales he'd heard about. He was eager to tell us about something he himself had experienced.

"Late one evening that October of 1981, when I was replacing the old wiring, I found myself on the fourth floor. There weren't as many rooms up there as on the other floors. I was still in the process of locating and pulling out the old knob and spool wiring and replacing it with Romex.

"It was time to quit for the day. From the silence, I knew everyone else had already left, but I thought maybe I could finish the job if I just stayed at it another hour or two. That's when I saw the door. I had to explore where it led, in case there was a closet or something with wiring that needed work too. I had been told to be thorough. The wooden door was held shut by a simple hook and eye on the right side. The hook really held tight in the eye, but I tapped upward on it with my hammer until it released its hold.

"As I pulled the door gently outward, the hinges creaked, and the door groaned as though objecting to being opened after the long time it had been left undisturbed. I found myself outside, on an area about eight feet square surrounded by a railing. I realized I must be standing where the cupola once had been. The view all around was breathtaking, and the air was so fresh. I decided to take my lunch breaks up there if I was asked to continue working on the house. But, for that day, it was time to call it quits. It was already past dusk.

"I stepped back into the interior fourth-story room, hooked the door again and gathered my tools. Because it was heavy and awkward to carry, I left the roll of Romex there on the floor. I put my electric drill in its handy carrying case, and I made sure I had swept up all the pieces of obsolete wiring and all the old fasteners and insulators and tossed them into the trash can I'd been using. Picking up my tool box and my drill set, I started down the narrow stairway to the third floor. On the second step from the bottom, I paused to catch my breath. That's when I heard it.

"No one else had been working that late. No one else was up on fourth floor when I started down. I'm sure of that. I listened intently for a few minutes trying to identify the sound. I could swear I heard what sounded like a drill turning up on the fourth floor—not a cordless drill, not an electric drill like mine, but one of those old-fashioned brace-and-bit drills that had to be turned by hand to make the bit chew away at the wood.

"I thought to myself, I haven't seen a hand drill in use for ages— and someone using one would have to have a flair for antique tools. Cordless drills were lots easier to manage. When I turned my good right ear toward the top of the stairway, I heard the noise more clearly. I went back up, having caught my breath sufficiently. I knew the sound came from the other side of that door I had just closed and hooked.

"It was dark out now. Not wanting to step outside again at that height in the dark, I turned to go back downstairs and head for home. As I did, I heard the drill again—and still from the other side of that hooked door. With all sorts of thoughts of dead generations of Kehoes and river-front pirates and funeral parlors and Halloween spooks running through my head, I hurried down the flights of stairs and almost ran to my pick-up out on Habersham. I was still shaking when I reached my own garage, parked the pickup and put my tool box and drill set on the garage work-bench. I stood there alone for a little while before I went on into the house. A few minutes later, while I was washing up, I told my wife I was

59

glad it was Friday night. I didn't tell her the rest of what I was thinking . . . that I was even happier I wouldln't have to return to the job until Monday. And on Monday, I wouldn't be the only one on the job. I'd make sure of that. And I sure would rethink my plan of taking lunch breaks out there on the other side of that door up on fourth floor."

⊰ 18 ⊱

Ghost Trains

As Lloyd finished up his story, we could all hear the sound of a train in the distance. We could hear the distinctive rumble of the engine and the plaintive wail of its horn at some crossing. Pine trees overhead sighed in the breeze, adding a note of melancholy to the Clearwater KOA next to the graveyard.

John, one of the campers who had not contributed up to that point, offered to tell a tale. In a fine southern drawl, he said he grew up in the small town of Jesup in Wayne County in southeast Georgia, about sixty miles southwest of Savannah. He said it was a quiet, peaceful town. While he lived there, he heard about what people called a "ghost train."

John said, "About eight miles out of Jesup, there's a light that shines down the railroad tracks. People commonly refer to it as the light from the ghost train, and folks there are used to calling it that.

"But that isn't it at all. It's not a high, straightforward beam like from a train engine's headlight, the kind of light one could expect to see there. It's more like a lantern, bobbing along down closer to the tracks.

"Many people have talked about this light. Some have reported seeing it. I've seen it, myself, on several occasions," John said.

"While I was growing up, I heard the story some folks told to explain the light. It seems that a railroad worker had been on the tracks one night when a train came bearing down on him. At that location, the tracks cut through a dense woods in an otherwise flat, sandy coastal plain. Whether he couldn't get off the tracks quickly enough or whether he intentionally stayed on the tracks isn't known.

"The engineer apparently didn't see the man. Or, if he did, perhaps he was too close for the train to come to a stop. It ain't easy to stop a hundred cars, you know. The inevitable happened: the train hit the man. One can imagine all sorts of results. In this case, the result was that the victim's head was knocked off.

"As if that wasn't horrible enough, or maybe because it was *so* horrible, a white light began to appear every night, just after nightfall. The light always seemed to be moving down the tracks. Again, it didn't look like a train's headlight, but more like the light of a lantern moving along a few feet above the ground.

"Perhaps the strangest thing about it is that no matter whether you're driving toward it on the road that runs parallel to the tracks or walking toward it right on the tracks, you never reach the light. It never gets closer. It stays there just out ahead of you somewhere, along the railroad tracks, on your own level where a person might be carrying it. The really odd thing is that no one ever sees anyone carrying the light.

"Rumor has it that the white light isn't from a train at all, but is carried by the unfortunate railroad worker who still walks down the tracks with his lantern. They say he's searching for his head.

"So there really is no ghost train at all, but I have to conclude that there must be a ghost."

"I want to point out," said the owner of the KOA, who happened to hear this story, "that Clearwater doesn't have trains running through it anymore. Clear Lake does, but that's to the east," and he pointed. "That train you and I just heard a few minutes ago . . . well, I sure don't know where it runs, but the nearest train in *that* direction is about thirty miles away."

"But that train sounded like it was at most a mile away," I said. "When the whistle blew, even the crickets got quiet."

Several others concurred.

"I know," said the owner. "I hear that train often. But even Clear Lake's line is at least eight miles off. Nothing between that one and the Soo Line that runs down by Kimball. Can't explain it."

So, maybe John's story didn't exactly include a ghost train, but, just maybe, all of us around my campfire had heard the real thing.

◁ 19 ▷

A Haunting Legacy

Mike Kennison, also a camper at the KOA, was interested in ecology. His work often took him to lakes, rivers, and even canals in the state of Florida. He was up in Minnesota on vacation, but he willingly told us about his work experience. Part of his job involved sampling water. He'd use hanging-glass, microscope slides at different depths for a specified time or lowered containers to trap water at varied depths. Then the samples were brought to the surface. Kennison recorded data about each sample: date, time, place, air and water temperatures, depths, and other variables.

Some tests he made on-site; others were conducted back at the lab. Then the identifying, counting, and recording of bits of life began. That work often lasted well into the night.

Kennison had never investigated a swamp. He wasn't sure he wanted to, but he saw it as a change. The surroundings would be different. Foreboding, maybe. But he knew that the environment was considerably varied and that any of its aspects could bring new information to light, maybe as yet unidentified microorganisms. He enjoyed plants of every kind, even those Floridians planted in their yards for color. If the swamp harbored water lilies, bromeliads and orchids, he'd find them. And he'd have his camera ready. And he told us his recent experiences in detail.

After Kennison and his partner had finished all their plans and preparations, they headed toward the Okefenokee Swamp, taking the most direct route—I-75 from Gainesville, then State Road 136. The swamp was located mostly in southeast Georgia, but spread into Florida's Baker County near the border. They would set up their field lab at the Stephen Foster Memorial Center located southwest of the swamp.

Kennison had seen some photos in a book he'd read about the swamp. He knew he'd be seeing cypress trees with their sometimes knobby "knees," and alligators if he watched for them. They'd still be active, before winter sent them into dormancy. He also knew that travel by boat would be slow and difficult at times because of the sluggish movement of the river and the tangled masses of vines in the wet areas. Travel on foot, sometimes on trembling peat bogs, would be slow and tiring. And hazardous. He'd have to mark his path to find the way safely back to the center.

Once the team reached the center, their plan was to alternate the sampling, testing, and recording of data. While Kennison went out to collect samples, his co-worker would stay at the minilab set up at one corner of the center's tourist parking lot.

The team's boat was a short, shallow, wide-bottomed aluminum craft meant to skim the surface of wet areas as smoothly as possible. At the same time, it would be light enough to portage when the water became too shallow.

The first night, both men had a good night's sleep in their van. "The moody swamp didn't get to you yet?" was the greeting Kennison heard in the morning from workers at the center.

On his way through breakfast and out to the boat, he heard the carillon in the tower playing. He recognized "Old Folks at Home," and he knew that had been Florida's state song since 1935. He wondered for a second what Georgia's state song was.

It was almost 9:00 on both his watch and on the tower clock. He heard a passerby say that the carillon played a lot of Stephen Foster's songs to honor him, and that "Old Folks at Home" was a song about the river and the people along it. Kennison reflected that he had heard that song often. He thought of the line, "Way down upon the Suwannee River . . ." but he thought of the word as Swanee, so it fit the rhythm of the line better.

"We'd better get our watches synchronized," Kennison told his partner. "You got 0900? I'll take the first run. Boat's ready. You all set in the field lab?"

All answers were in the affirmative, and the two parted. Kennison headed up the Suwannee toward the swamp.

The swamp was dark, dreary, and foreboding, even if it did provide an ever-changing panorama of plant and animal life.

He noticed by late morning that the murky, almost black water with a tangle of hollies, blackberries, and vines along the banks phased into open areas where he could see the trees reflecting in the quiet water of what resembled little lakes. Gray Spanish moss draped the live oaks and magnolias like a decorator's finished display, and the water reflected it, making a shadowy, spectral-like enclosure around the boat.

As he reached the third sampling location, Kennison glanced at his watch: 11:30 already. Occasionally, he could still hear the carillon playing its plaintive tunes, but he'd soon be too far away to hear familiar lyrics and melodies.

The planned routine was working well. One collected the samples by boat while the other identified, counted, and recorded the data with the help of the lab's special microscope and computer. One man always had to remain in the mini-van to insure safety and security for the equipment as well as the whole project.

On the fifth day, it was again Kennison's turn to collect the samples. That was the day he heard the flute music. It played simple tunes, like those a young child would play. There was something eerie about the flute, though, and Kennison thought of the times when his daughter had to learn how to handle sharps and flats on her keyboard. Then he remembered reading that Stephen Foster could play a flute when he was four, on his way to becoming a very capable musician. But he was dead . . . long ago, of course. So, who was playing a flute here in the swamp?

Soon Kennison heard the carillon playing. *That's more like it*, he thought. *None of this kids' stuff.* But a time check told him it was playing on the quarter-hour, not the usual hour and half-hour. That was confusing. Was his watch off?

Later that day, Kennison struggled the boat through a tangle of spiny greenbrier vines. He used the pole, but still he couldn't get any leverage. He worked to push the mass away and finally succeeded. It wasn't long before he had reached a large clearing at the middle of the swamp near the headwaters of the Suwannee River.

Here the cypress trees stood tall and were reflected in the dark water, their knees multiplied by their quivering images on the water's surface.

The swamp fascinated him. This was an entirely different place from what he was used to. Woodpeckers announced their presence by hammering in the high branches. Herons played statues at the edge of the water. The showy blooms of the water lilies floated over the dark water. He couldn't believe the fresh beauty around him. He spotted the bright leaves of a tupelo tree almost hidden by Spanish moss draping its branches. Using the pole to steady the boat, he paused to sit down and take it all in.

He was in a dark area, surrounded by thick vegetation, yet in navigable water that was calm and mirror-like. Masses of moss in the trees reflected in the water. It hung like curtains almost to the bow of the boat. The reflection made him feel he was in the middle of it all—the moss, the trees, the swamp—near the very heart of the river. He felt almost smothered, as if the moss was taking its nourishment from the air he needed to breathe. He thought of the resurrection fern that grew in the live oaks and magnolia trees. It looked dead. Then it soaked up the rain and became refreshed and healthy again.

In the middle of all this, deep in the swamp and closed in on all sides by trees, vines, and hanging moss, he heard it. The music. It couldn't be coming from the tower. He was too far away now. And it was the wrong hour for it. It didn't stop and wait for a half hour to go by. It started with simple tunes played on a flute but kept going, getting more involved and interwoven, something like echoes bouncing in a cave.

He picked out tunes he knew: "Oh! Susanna." "Gentle Annie." "Laura Lee." "Jeanie with the Light Brown Hair." "Nelly Bly."

These were played with tenderness, sadness, homesickness, a longing for warmth and love. Kennison remembered how Stephen Foster's life had ended: His spendy ways. His broken marriage. His death, alone in New York City at a young age with only a few cents in his pocket.

Sometimes the tunes seemed to come from the trees above, as if the sad songs had been plaintively whistled by lonely birds. Sometimes the music came from the water. Kennison could have sworn someone was teasing him . . . swimming alongside the boat and singing, yet out of sight. But he told himself that was stupid, considering that the alligators were sometimes unpredictable. And he hardly thought anyone would be on the peat bog, the masses of sphagnum moss underfoot cushioning the melancholy of the songs like a giant sponge.

As the day grew later and darker, Kennison was forced to start back. As he turned the boat around, his glance took in movement. He was sure something moved up in the trees. *Up in that mass of drapery,* he thought. "Okay, whatever or whoever you are, I'll get you on film!" And his camera flashed and clicked.

The music sorted out into other recognizable songs, this time sung and accompanied by a banjo. "Open Thy Lattice, Love" was the first one. He wished the Spanish moss lattice would open up and go away so he could move the boat more easily. Then he heard "Come Where My Love Lies Dreaming" and he realized how alone he, too, felt there in the swamp. Last, "Beautiful Dreamer" was sung though it joined the others as they alternated or combined into a well-orchestrated blend of nostalgia and sadness and loneliness.

The moody swamp has finally gotten to me, he realized. *What else could it be? There's no one else around. I'm alone with my thoughts. Or am I?*

He gave thought to the idea that he was going nuts. With that, he put the boat in motion and started back the way he had come.

No one believed him, of course. Not his partner. Not the tourists. Not the staff at the center, though they looked him in the eye and asked just where he was when he heard the songs. Not his fellow-researchers. Not his wife and daughters. Not until the film was developed, and they asked what that was up in the Spanish moss in that one picture.

There was the answer to the source of the music. Clearly outlined. A shadowy figure hovering in the tree branches, as much in the hanging moss as in the trees, tenderly holding his banjo and singing his heart out, "way down upon the Suwannee River."

Kennison had heard the legends since his return from the swamp. The gist of it was that, though Foster had never seen the Suwannee nor the swamp where the river begins its meandering before he composed his songs about it, he felt the spirit of his music so keenly that he lingered on in the area where his songs lived on, perpetuated by the center and the faithful carillon. And by men like Kennison and his work partner, and fellas like us at that KOA camp in Minnesota who listened to the story.

⊰ 20 ⊱

Restless Souls

John Horton's story can best be told as he told it to me. He told it well, and as I listened it was easy to imagine hearing him tell it, guitar in hand, to an audience. He was known as the cowboy poet in the KOA campground at Rapid City, South Dakota, where we met over a pancake breakfast. I invited him to come to the campfire that night and share his story with whoever came to listen. He agreed.

"Near Appomattox, Virginia," he began that evening, "after hitchhiking all day, I stopped to camp under a cluster of trees at the edge of a small valley. The year was 1956, so I was a lot younger. I was naught more than a kid out looking for adventure. As I built a small fire, I recalled vaguely that I had once read about what had happened during the Civil War. It was not quite a hundred years earlier, in fact, that the Confederates surrendered to the federal army on April 9, 1865, at the old Appomattox Court House nearby. The site later became a national historical park.

"Once the fire was crackling and the coffee was boiling, I warmed up something to eat with it. It was probably beans, the old tried and true camper's supper mainstay. After I ate, I rested, leaning back against the trunk of a sturdy oak tree. I lit up my pipe and just sat there a while, watching a little haze that hung over the valley.

"There were a few lights in the dwellings in the distance. Not much traffic, but I could hear an occasional vehicle go by out on the highway. I unrolled my pack, smoothed out my bed and went to sleep.

"Shortly before dawn, I was awakened by the sound of human cries and gunfire. There, on that valley floor, I watched men and boys, in blue and gray, fight a small skirmish. I have no idea how long it lasted, but as the sun rose above the rolling hills, the men retired from the field, and the light haze again covered the place where they had fought.

"I got up from where I had slept on my bedroll and I walked down and inspected the field. I figured I had come during some kind of reenactment. But there was no sign that anyone had actually been there that morning. The shouts and gunfire had been so real, though. And I could smell the acrid smoke from their gunfire.

"Later that day, as I walked along the road, an old man in a '46 Ford gave me a ride into Appomattox. When I told him where I had camped, he smiled and asked me, with his distinctive southern drawl, 'Did the boys come out to fight?'

"I was startled. I related what I had seen and heard and smelled. He just smiled, then said, 'Some day, I hope their souls can rest and never have to fight again.'

"I rode with him for twenty miles. There was no indication that he was other than a human, living person, but I had to wonder. He said he had seen that battle many times in his sixty years in the same area. He let me off, and I went on my way.

"I've been back there three times since, but I've never seen that battle staged again. I even camped in the same spot a couple times, but I saw nothing. I figure it was not meant to be replayed for me."

◄ 21 ►

A Thud and a Scream

I made a trip to Judge C. R. Magney State Park in northeast Minnesota. Just off Lake Superior on the Brule River, this state park offers quiet campsites, invigorating nature walks, and a mystery of its own. After a mile-long hike up hill and down, campers arrive at the site of the Devil's Kettle. The Brule River has a waterfall here. Half the water tumbles down a cascade of rocks in white froth before winding its way to Lake Superior. The other half of the river's flow, however, falls into a huge stone kettle and is never seen again. Researchers intent on finding out where the water goes have dumped dyes, ping-pong balls, and various other things into that kettle's mouth, but they never show up again. Not in the frothy water below the falls, not farther down stream, not even out in Lake Superior. Quite literally, no one knows where that water goes. It's a mystery.

While toasting marshmallows at my campfire in the campgrounds of the park and contemplating the mystery of the Devil's Kettle, a woman with a pronounced Jersey accent asked if I was the one who had put the notice on the camp bulletin board about wanting to hear ghost stories for a book. I told her I was indeed that person and offered her a stick to roast her own marshmallows. She laughed and pulled a chocolate bar and a packet of graham crackers from her bag and sat down.

Her name was Carrie, and she told me about her experience. She had walked the few blocks to the library, hoping to find enough sources for her research paper. She was beginning to take an interest in history, even after thinking since sixth grade that anything historical had to be boring. Her parents loved to visit historical sites in New Jersey and made an outing out of each trip, packing tasty picnic lunches and encouraging Carrie to invite a friend along. That made history a little more tolerable, Carrie conceded, but now it wasn't summer. She was well into the second quarter of her senior year of high school, so she would have to do her research at the Bernardsville Public Library. She arrived about 8:30, wishing it hadn't gotten so far into the evening. The library would likely close before she finished.

Sandi, the reference librarian, sat at her desk, almost hidden by stacks of books to be checked in and reshelved. It looked like it had been a busy day for her. She pushed her bifocals up on her nose as she looked up and stared at Carrie, probably wondering what this skinny, blonde, high school student wanted now. She'd been in before.

The topic Carrie had chosen from the teacher's recommended list was, "The Part the Vealtown Tavern played in the Revolutionary War." It seemed like a dumb subject, but she had been absent the day before when the assignment was made, and other classmates had snapped up all the more interesting topics. When she repeated what she had to research to Sandi, expecting a long sigh and a roll of her eyes, the woman's face instead lit up. The moment before she had been tired looking with stacks of books to process and almost wincing at the idea that Carrie might need her help. Before Carrie knew it, Sandi had bounced up and trotted off, calling over her shoulder, "Well, you've come to the right place, all right! This building used to be the Vealtown Tavern!"

Then Sandi almost shoved Carrie into the reference section, handed her several books as she pulled them from the shelves at light speed, and piled on some papers from the vertical file. Grinning, she said, "Here's what you'll need. But now you're on your own. I've got other work to do!" and left Carrie with an armload of sources and surrounded by the zillions of shelved books in the stacks.

Carrie staggered to a table. Fortunately most of the tables were vacant at that late hour, so she didn't have to stumble far. She put everything down on the table, sat and browsed through the table of contents of a couple of the books. Then she spied a reprint of an article on New Jersey folklore, from a Princeton publication Sandi had given her. Seeing that it was fairly short, she began reading it and making a few notes on the legal pad she had brought for that purpose.

"There!" she told herself. "I've got the source listed, so I won't have to come back later to make my bibliography." A previous paper had been docked points when she had failed to note sources.

She began to read the two columns of New Jersey folklore and almost dozed off. When the head librarian walked by, clicking her heels on the tiled floor, she jerked to attention and forced herself to read on.

"During the Revolution the building now occupied by the Bernardsville Public Library housed the Vealtown Tavern, owned and operated by a Captain Parker and his daughter, Phyllis. After General Washington moved his troops to Pluckemin, following the Battle of Princeton, the tavern became a gathering place for American officers traveling between the camp and Washington's winter headquarters in Morristown."

Well, okay, Carrie thought. *That gets me into the time of the Revolutionary War, so it gets me started. I wonder who this Phyllis was.* There was no physical description of her in the article, so Carrie tried to imagine her as a petite young woman with long, dark hair, snapping black eyes, and maybe a quick temper when she was upset. That way, when she wrote about her, she would seem more real.

She read on, and found out that Phyllis was engaged to young Dr. Byram, a boarder at the tavern, who had started his practice as a physician only a few months earlier. Carrie decided to think of him as trim, tall, and friendly. She let her imagination fill in the details. He had been friendly and pleasant to everyone he came in contact with at Vealtown, and certainly so to all at the tavern. He was beginning to be accepted in the town and frequently was called out on a case, at any hour of day or night.

The article went on to say that in January of 1777, a General Wayne and his men asked for rooms at the tavern. While they were being accommodated, Dr. Byram excused himself to go to his room. But the next morning, both he and his horse were gone.

Carrie thought, *This kind of history isn't so bad. There seems to be a mystery shaping up. Maybe a love story, too.* She read on, taking a few notes in her own words as she did. Everyone thought the doctor had gone to answer a sick call during the night, until General Wayne told Captain Parker that his packet of orders was missing.

Captain Parker was questioned. He swore that no Tories were in Vealtown, that everyone was a life-long resident—everyone except Dr. Byram. When the officers asked for a description of the doctor, Parker produced a miniature portrait of Byram that the doctor had given Phyllis.

Carrie made a note to refresh her memory on who the Tories were, but she was enjoying the article. It next revealed that General Wayne recognized the man in the photo as . . . not Dr. Byram, but Aaron Wilde, a Tory spy.

According to the article, the general and his troops caught Wilder ("Byram") later that day. He had been seen exchanging information with British officers near Princeton. He was easily recognized, as his reddish hair and small moustache and his roan horse had already become a familiar sight in the area as he made medical calls. People who were questioned by the officers helpfully pointed out the direction he had ridden. As a result, Wilde was hanged, and his body, sealed in a wooden casket, was delivered to Captain Parker for burial.

Parker, of course, wanted to save his daughter any sorrow or embarrassment, so she was not told about the theft of military papers or the hanging, just that Dr. Byram had died. As yet, however, he had not told Phyllis anything.

The box arrived that evening. Soldiers marched in through the kitchen, set it on the floor of the tavern's dining room and marched out. Though she had not been told of it, Phyllis must have sensed the presence of her lover. That's when pandemonium broke loose. Phyllis, possibly having heard the clomping sounds of the soldiers' footsteps, went to the dining room near midnight and, with a hatchet, split the box open and recognized her fiancé. Guests were awakened by the racket, and, as they ran to the dining room, they heard a prolonged, heart-rending scream. There was Phyllis, kneeling next to the destroyed box and quite hysterical. It's said that she never did recover.

Carrie was so absorbed in the story's events and outcome that she was startled when the librarian clicked by to remind her that it was closing time. She said to Carrie, "If you need to check out any of these materials, the time to do that is now."

Before Carrie left for home, she quickly checked out a book to explain to her who the Tories were, and a magazine article that repeated much of what she had just read from the Princeton publication. By the time she devoured a goodly snack in the kitchen at home, and read the rest of the story in her own room, it was close to midnight. She learned that in the 1800s the Vealtown Tavern was turned into a private residence. A series of owners and occupants were disturbed by unexplained sounds such as heavy footsteps, swishing skirts, and hurried, light tiptoeing on the stairs at night. But the worst experience of all was on one night in January 1977, exactly 100 years after Byram's death and his beloved's undoing. First, the current occupants heard the heavy footsteps as if someone marched through the kitchen and into the dining room. They heard the *thunk* of a heavy object being set down, and more marching boots parading back through the kitchen and out the door. A little later, they heard a thunderous crash and the sounds of splintering wood, followed by a "piercing scream" and "sobbing moans which faded into the night."

Carrie was thankful that she was safe in her own bed in her own room when she read that, but it caused her spine to crawl nonetheless. But she was just curious enough to think it might be interesting to go back to the library on January 29 for the "ghost watch" the library's board of directors was planning in order to honor the bicentennial of the spirit's appearance. The magazine article ended with that information. Her light still on, Carrie drifted off to sleep thinking about it. And she almost cracked her head on the ceiling when her door opened slowly and a gentle voice asked, "Carrie, aren't you asleep yet? It's after midnight."

"After that," Carrie told me as she squashed a flaming marshmallow between two bits of graham cracker, "history has seemed less like work and more like a mystery waiting to be solved."

I told her about the Devil's Kettle and how the waterfall disappeared down a chute into oblivion, and she smiled. "That's why I came here. I wanted to see it for myself."

◄ 22 ►

A Thumping on the Porch

A little while later, after all the marshmallows, chocolate, and graham crackers were gone except for a lingering stickiness, Carrie's travel companion, Janet, found us and joined the fire. When she learned we were telling spooky stories, she bounced on her log, eager to tell one. Janet told us that, in sixth grade, she lived with her grandparents, Arthur and Ethel. They lived in Seaside Heights, New Jersey. For a number of years until she married, that was Janet's home.

"Grandpa and Grandma bought the house in the early 1940s," Janet said. "It was a two-story frame, built high up on the coast, so its basement was above ground level. That explained why there were not two or three, but ten steps leading up to the front porch, but with the possibility of hurricanes on the coast, it kept the basement from filling with water."

"I remember counting the steps as I climbed them. Let's see, it went like this: 'Two, four, where's the door. Six, eight, I'll be late. Nine, ten, I'm here again!' as I raced up them two at a time and crossed the porch to the door."

Janet said she liked the old house and liked living with her grandparents. But she still remembers hearing strange sounds she couldn't figure out, especially during the time she was a teenager. When she visited later, she also heard the unexplainable sounds.

"They made quite an impression on me. At first they scared me, but I got used to them and, like a young detective, tried to track them down. I thought of old sea captains and pirates on the coast, and everything else I could think of that fit the scene.

"The sounds were heavy steps, as if a well-built man was coming up the steps and across the porch to the door. He took the steps one at a time, though! But when we went out and looked, there was never anyone out on the porch. The mystery was sort of intriguing.

"Grandpa and Grandma never wanted to talk about it. I never knew for sure if they heard the sounds or not. But all of that just added to the mystery, for me."

The Hurleys continued to live there after Janet was married and left for her new home with her husband.

A few years later, Grandpa Hurley had some trouble with his legs. Eventually, he had to have one amputated. After that, things didn't go well for him, and he died.

After Arthur's death, the house with all its space and all its memories was just too big and lonely for Ethel. She eventually sold the place and made arrangements to live on a rotating basis with her two daughters and with Janet. They helped her get things sorted and packed and moved.

But the sounds didn't move out with her. In a letter from the people who had been next-door neighbors, Ethel heard about it. The new owners, the Porters from up in Maine, were disturbed by sounds like footsteps on the porch, day and night. And the sounds changed. When the Porters heard the thumping, it was as if a one-legged man —or maybe a man with one good leg and a stump—was thumping up the steps and across the porch.

On her next visit with Janet, Grandma said that the Porters had abruptly moved out, leaving the house vacant—except, perhaps, for its mysterious occupant who continued to clamber up the steps one at a time and thump across the porch to visit an old haunt.

◅ 23 ▻

Confront the Hovering Spirit

Not content with only one ghost story, Janet started right in on another as loons called out on Lake Superior and the Brule River gurgled past the campgrounds.

The part of New Jersey where Janet and her husband, Jim, lived was Toms River and had once been inhabited by Indians. People knew that from archaeological digs in the area and their own normal, everyday digging such as setting a post for a martin house or a mailbox. Whenever they dug, bones would come up.

Janet and Jim, newlyweds, lived a couple blocks down the street from Janet's mother's house. The young couple's home was fairly new, but they never felt alone there. They sensed a presence—as if they never really had the house to themselves. They wondered if it was because of the bones. Their abundance did give people a creepy feeling.

The young couple had that feeling as well, in any part of the house. They felt almost as if someone was watching them. It made them very uncomfortable.

In that neighborhood, there was a tradition. Everyone came in for a birthday party or a holiday get-together. When they gathered at Janet and Jim's, they got used to strange happenings. When they were downstairs, they would hear footsteps in the upstairs hall. It was a heavy step, as if a man was walking down the carpeted hall. One time, everyone was downstairs in the rec room when Jim heard it. He quieted the others, and they all heard the footsteps. All the men ran up the basement steps to check out the noise. They found nothing. It was a little upsetting

78

—enough that one couple that lived next door even ran over to their house to make sure their children were all right. Everyone was baffled. They all talked about it.

Janet had read books on the subject. She had learned that if one encountered something like a presence or a feeling over a long time, someone was trying to tell the person something.

That night she remembered that once, some time after her father died, she'd had especially strong feelings. Her mother had remarried by then. Janet was alone down in the laundry room of her mother's and stepfather's home when she felt like someone else was there. She burst out, "What? What do you want? Leave me alone!"

When she told her mom about it, her mom said, "Well, I guess Dad (Janet's stepfather) took care of that, too!"

And that was it. The strong feelings of a presence in the house never came back. As if "Dad" had willed the confrontation to get rid of the spirit, thinking it might have been that of Janet's real father hovering protectively over her.

But whose spirit was hovering over Janet and Jim's home now? Did it have some connection to the bones? Was someone lurking there, waiting for his or her bones to be dug up and moved to a more comfortable burial place? Did he announce his presence by the footsteps, at times when he could get the attention of the whole neighborhood? Janet never knew, but, when they moved out of the area, the unease vanished, and life proceeded on a much happier note.

But that wasn't the end of the story. Janet said, "After Grandpa died in that house in Seaside Heights, Mom and Dad took Grandma Hurley home with them to their own house in Toms River."

The house had a combined living and dining room with a kitchen beyond. From there, you either went down into the family room or up to the bedroom area.

"One evening," Janet said, "Grandma was upstairs in her bedroom. Mom was in the kitchen doing dishes. She went down to the family room to get the ashtrays, to finish the cleanup.

"The family room was almost all windows. Mother looked out the window ahead of the stairs and over to the right. She saw her father smiling at her. Plain as day. Several minutes later she could still see him there. The reflection from the glass made it seem as if he was sitting in the chair to the right of the stairs.

"After staring at the visage for another full minute, Mom went up to find Dad and tell him what she saw. He went down and looked, but Grandpa wasn't there anymore. Mother felt that Grandpa had come back to let her know he'd be back again for Grandma."

Even this wasn't the end. Janet continued by telling us that, when she was a young girl, her father was in the Coast Guard. He died in Philadelphia when she was nine years old.

Four years later, when Janet was close to thirteen, he appeared to her. She said to him, "Can I help you?"

This happened periodically, Janet said, especially when she was troubled about something. And it seemed to happen in that limbo between sleeping and waking when real and not real could get muddled in the mind.

When Janet was fifteen, her mother remarried. The next time Janet's father "appeared" to Janet in that in-between time, she asked him, "Did you know Mom was married again?"

His answer: "I know. I still love her, and I want her to be happy."

Normally when he appeared, Janet could see him only from his waist up, as if she was seated and she couldn't see below her own height. Or as if she lay in bed and could only see the upper part of his body without fully waking and sitting up in bed. It was hard to explain. She sometimes thought maybe he was seated, as in a patrol boat, and could communicate with her from there without stepping over the side of the boat.

The years passed. When Janet was eighteen, she was planning to marry. The night before the day of the wedding, her father came to her again. He said, "Is there anything I can do to help you?"

Janet said, "I'm glad you came. I wanted to tell you I'm getting married tomorrow."

Very simply, he said, "Yes, I know."

He never appeared to Janet again. It was as if during her adolescent years, he wanted to continue to be helpful, to be a part of her experience and help in any way he could. But now he knew she would be all right and would be taken care of by someone who loved her. She wouldn't need him any longer.

◄ 24 ►

Josie Never Liked Flowers

It was getting late by now, and Minnesota's state bird, the mosquito, had made a rather nasty appearance. We built up the fire a bit to stave them off, and Janet told us about her mother's friend Josie, who didn't, apparently, like flowers. In fact, she hated them in no uncertain terms. They were a bother. They made a mess. They made her sneeze. Some of them actually smelled awful. And the water in the vases—if you left it for even a couple of days without changing it . . . whew!

Other than her dislike for flowers—and most people would accept that either as Josie's idiosyncrasy or as a kind of twisted reasoning—Josie, a stocky Italian lady, had a heart of gold.

When her time came to die, there was a huge crowd for the visitation at the funeral home as well as for the service at the church.

Besides her four children and their families and Josie's many siblings and their spouses and offspring, all the townspeople came to show their love and respect for the woman who had been nice to everyone and had done a lot of thoughtful little things for them.

The only people who didn't have thoughts for Josie were some members of the garden club. Josie had made it known to them that she didn't feel as they did about having a lot of flowers around. She told them off about the time and energy they spent on their flowerbeds. "And for what?" she had asked. "Come cold weather and that first frost, they're just gonna die anyway. What a waste!"

But when Josie died, no one thought *not* to give flowers. They were all over the place. There were so many at the funeral home that dozens of arrangements were hung on brackets or by S-hooks against the walls. A huge bouquet weighed down the lid of the casket, of course. If Josie could have seen or smelled them, she would have had a fit.

Janet said, "My Mom was usually not of a real calm and cool disposition. But this time, she surprised me.

"We were at the visitation the evening before the funeral. I sat beside her while the pastor did a Scripture reading and a short prayer service. He was saying something complimentary about Josie, too— about how good she had been to everyone, how thoughtful she had been. He said, 'Your presence here and all these flowers given in her memory out of the love in your hearts are a fitting tribute to our dear, departed Josie." Then someone sneezed.

About then, Janet and her mother probably had the same thought. The minister didn't know Josie very well. Not about the flowers, anyway.

No sooner had we all heard the sneeze on top of the minister's remarks, while that thought about the minister not knowing Josie very well had entered my mind, than the arrangements started sliding off the wall and the casket and down onto the carpeted floor.

Janet finished telling the story: "Mom turned to me and said very, very quietly and calmly, 'You know, Janet, Josie really hated flowers.'"

⊰ 25 ⊱

Flying Dishes in Toms River

Sitting within view of the Brule River brought up another story from the well that was Janet's life, and she proceeded to tell it next, even as she recalls it.

It had been a while since she and Jim had managed to spend an evening with Barbara and Levi, their long-time friends. But as Janet and Jim reached the porch, Barbara opened the door before Janet reached for the knocker.

Hugs and warm greetings put Janet and Jim at ease even as they were ushered into the living room, where Levi had cocktails ready on the side table.

Jim was already asking, "What's for supper? Smells good!" Janet heard Barb answer, "Meat loaf." Janet's mind was occupied just then with thinking, *Auntie's here as always, here in her frame on the wall, her eyes as steely as ever.* Janet remembered what Barb had told her about those eyes. "They seem to come right out of the portrait and follow me wherever I go," Barb had said, "and I always feel a deep chill when I look up at Auntie there on the living room wall. Or when I dust the frame and the mantle below it, for that matter. Makes me not want to dust it at all."

Barb and Levi's house, one of the older ones on Water Street in Toms River, stood impressively on the mainland, overlooking the river itself above where it dumped into Barnegat Bay. The bay flowed, by way of Barnegat Inlet, into the Atlantic. Across the bay lay Seaside Heights, on the narrow four-block-wide strip of land across from the New Jersey mainland.

The two couples hadn't seen each other since Janet left Toms River, though they had kept in touch by mail. This particular evening, Janet and Jim looked forward to a real good catching-up visit. "And a good meal, I hope!" Jim had said emphatically as they had approached the porch. "A whole day of boating and fishing left me with a whopper of an appetite."

Remembering other times as she sipped her martini, Janet caught herself wondering if Barbara knew how to make meat loaf. She wandered out to the dining room. Levi followed, wondering what Janet was up to.

Their presence in the dining room seemed to activate some kind of vigorus energy. From the copper dry-sink at the bottom of the tall cupboard, Barbara's lovely bone china dishes were suddenly airborne.They weren't sliding off the shelves into the dry-sink below, but were flying from it and over it in all directions and onto the floor.

Janet and Levi hardly needed to call out to the other two. The clatter of the dishes was enough to summon the dead. As Jim came from the living room, he was saying, "What a racket!" But no one else heard him.

All four stood watching and dodging the flying plates and cups and saucers. Janet suddenly remembered the last time she had been in the house and the bad, frightening feelings she couldn't explain or overcome. When it all came to a stop this time, Janet knew the evening she had so looked forward to enjoying had turned into a disaster.

Another recollection flashed into her memory—one Barbara had written about at Christmas. "I was upstairs," the letter said, "when I heard music. It was piano music, coming from downstairs." But no one else was in the house that night. And Jingo, Barb's Siamese cat, wasn't musically talented. Yet the melancholy strains of "Clair de Lune" floated up to her from the player piano in the living room.

Was Auntie resentful of Barbara for interfering in her nephew's life—or for coming between her and her favorite nephew? Was she resentful toward Levi for marrying Barb and bringing her here to this house, where Auntie still "lived on"? Was she showing her feelings by bringing them to the notice of good friends? And was it somehow significant that there were no children in the house—not on the night the dishes flew, or any other night?

As Janet finished her story, she left us with questions and a chill that seeped into us like the mist rolling in off Superior.

◄ 26 ►

A Nonexistent Stairway

Coming back down Highway 61 from Judge C. R. Magney State Park, I found it natural to pause at some of the other state parks located at other rivers that emptied into Superior. I visited Temperance River State Park, named because, unlike most of the rivers that entered Lake Superior, the Temperance River had no sand bar. Okay, somebody should have seen that coming.

Split Rock Lighthouse offered great views of the lake. I had my lunch there before heading south to pull in at Gooseberry Falls, where I had reservations for the night. After walks along the river and over the bridges that span the churning water, after visiting the falls and being impressed with the beauty of the area, I settled into my campsite for the evening. As usual, I had posted an invitation to anyone wishing to share ghost stories. Also, as usual, a number of folks took me up on the offer and joined me at my campfire. I usually liked to have some small bits of refreshment available to my guests. This day I had stopped at a lovely bakery in Lutsen, so I offered people chewy chocolate-chip cookies. One of the first people to arrive was a woman in her sixties who had come up to Gooseberry Falls from Duluth for the weekend, taking a kind of mini-vacation from a demanding journalist job. Anna had seen my notice and liked the idea of company.

"This happened to me long ago," Anna told me as she nibbled the proffered cookie. "Right after I was married, actually. Smitty and I had thought to start our honeymoon at a lovely B&B in Duluth. We had just gone through maybe the longest day of our lives with little sleep the night before. The preparation for the wedding, the ceremony itself, then the reception, which had lasted from two in the afternoon to nearly two the next morning. We had dragged ourselves to the B&B and sat down on a settee waiting for the manager's daughter to come down for our bags."

Suddenly, tired as he was, Smitty sat up straight and looked toward the stairway. Anna, noticing his sudden movement, looked up and asked, "What, Smitty? What's the matter?"

"Dunno. Guess I dozed off. But I heard someone on the stairs. Did you just come down?"

"We haven't gone up yet. I was here all the while. Maybe you fell asleep. It has been a long day. Maybe it was the daughter coming to get us." And with that, Jan snuggled against her young husband.

Their settee faced the stairs to the second floor. "Wake me if I fall asleep, will you?" Anna said with a yawn. "I wouldn't want to miss anything," Anna winked and offered him a sly grin.

The entry parlor was perfectly quiet for the next few minutes. Smitty leaned over to kiss his bride just as Anna sat up. The back corner of her side of the settee nearly knocked him out as it bounced forward.

When the surprise was over, Smitty asked, "What was that for? Is the honeymoon over?"

"Of course not, Smitty. I thought I heard someone on the steps just now."

"But, Anna, look! There's no one there. And I was facing that way all the while you had your eyes closed. Except just now. But . . . besides, there's no one else down here."

"You didn't hear anything? Well, the noises were sort of faint. Like they came from the den, not right here in front of us."

"You thought so, too? I mean—you heard footsteps on the stairs, too, like I did? Only not on these stairs?"

"Yeah. But there aren't any other steps that I can see."

A moment later a woman clomped down the stairs and approached them. "Your room is ready for you now," she said pleasantly. "Sorry for the delay. We want our newlyweds to be particularly comfortable. Upstairs at the end of the hall. Enjoy your stay."

She handed the couple their keys and headed down the hall to the kitchen. Anna and Smitty climbed the carpeted stairs and found their room at the end of the hall. Candles had been lit and soft music played. A bottle of champagne chilled in an ice bucket and two champagne flutes decorated with ribbons awaited them on the coffee table. Delectable treats—hors d'oeuvres, little cakes, and a variety of crackers—had been laid out for them.

They felt refreshed and enjoyed a tasty snack and sips of bubbly.

"We must be getting the jitters. And it's no wonder, just the two of us awake in this big old house by the lake."

Nothing disturbed the two for the rest of the weekend, the extent of their brief honeymoon.

Monday morning after a delightful if hurried breakfast, the couple rode to work together. Smitty dropped Anna off in front of the *Duluth Herald* building.

Anna only had half a day's work. The next day, she would be on duty most of the night, or at least until the morning paper was "put to bed." Thinking about that, and not remembering what they had in their refrigerator, she grabbed a jug of milk at the corner store at noon before she took a taxi to the couple's new home, one of the big houses above downtown.

The house was so quiet that Jan found herself thinking about those sounds they had both heard at the B&B. She even caught herself looking toward the stairs again and again as she "picked up" in the front part of the house, sorted cards needing thank-yous, and tried to organize the small mountain of gifts they had received.

Late that afternoon, Anna whipped up a chocolate cake mix and baked it. More a journalist than a homemaker, she could at least pretend. Just as she smoothed out the last knife full of canned fudge frosting, she about hit the ceiling. There was that sound again! The exact same sound she and Smitty had heard in the B&B, though it was miles away. She turned so fast she knocked the empty cake pan off the counter. When she heard Smitty's, "Hi, honey. What's for supper?" she realized all she had heard was her husband coming up the back porch steps.

"Oh! It's just you!"

His face fell. "*Just* me? Who were you expecting? Why so jumpy? And what's this frosting doing on the floor?"

Anna was happy to have him home. Yet the haunting feeling was still there, the prickly uncertainty. The sense of a presence, yet seeing no one. The thought of someone, some stranger, perhaps, being in the house when they were and weren't home.

This went on for several months until both Smitty and Anna were about ready to move out.

"This is just too much," Anna ventured one night. "Footsteps, day and night on steps that aren't even there! It just can't be! I've had it!"

"What did you say? Oh, hey, honey, maybe you've got it! I mean, when you think of footsteps on nonexistent steps . . . maybe that's it! Steps that were there *once*, but aren't there anymore!"

When the confusion cleared, Smitty's thought led to a thorough, systematic search of the house. They tapped walls and studied the interiors of closets, looking for clues.

At the back of the house, near the porch but on a wall in the den, straight horizontal lines ascended evenly to the second floor level. There, a railing stretched across above the highest mark.

Jan had been wondering why the railing was there instead of a solid wall. And as they felt the ridges left on the wall by numerous earlier paint jobs, Jan and Smitty were baffled. It truly looked as if a second stairs had been boarded over.

Not long after this discovery, they had a phone call. "Hi, this is Sheila, your realtor. I just wanted to touch base with you. How do you like your new home? Do you still think it's too big for just the two of you, or do you like having lots of room like I thought?"

In the course of the conversation, Smitty asked Sheila about the lines on the den wall.

"Oh. Funny you should mention that. Yes, there used to be a stairway there. The Clarks renovated the house about fifteen years ago. They didn't see a need for two stairways, so, in order to have a larger den, they moved those stairs to the back part of the house—the part that the Smiths tore down when they bought it. That was shortly before the Hendersons bought it—the people who lived there just before you. One of those families had an ancestor who was a pirate long ago . . . but why did you ask about the lines? There's never been any leakage or anything. Is there a problem?"

"Oh, we just wondered . . . we heard . . . uh . . . ."

"I didn't mention it to you, because I thought there was no reason to."

Sheila's information explained the marks on the wall and the stairway but not the mysterious sounds of someone ascending and descending those nonexistent stairs, day and night. Nor why the sounds had started at the B&B. And pirates? Anna and Smitty stayed in the old house several years, then moved to a new house they had built in a new development near Thunderbird Mall. But, even in a brand new house, one that never had an obsolete stairway, the sounds continued. Someone insisted on following them around and climbing stairs that weren't there. Still, Anna and Smitty made peace with the spirit, called, "Hello," when they heard the steps or, "Knock it off!" if the tromping came late at night.

Interestingly, while making a garden in the backyard the next spring after they moved in, Anna found a large gold coin. Whoever this pirate ancestor was to someone they didn't even know, at least he paid his rent.

‹ 27 ›

Blue Lights Next Door

Ken, who has a last name so complicated in its spelling that I can't begin to guess how to pronounce it, also stopped by at my Gooseberry Falls campfire. Ken had come to tell me about his unusual experience. In fact, he told about several incidents or phenomena that seem to be tied together into an otherwise unexplainable whole. They all make their contribution to his ghost story.

The setting was a usually very small, quiet resort town on the Massachusetts coast near Newburyport. Salisbury Beach had seedy, sea-weathered buildings rented out to summer vacationers with perhaps less money than those who secured the big homes and resorts of Martha's Vineyard, but it was a popular place nonetheless.

In one of these structures Ken had made his home for the summer. It was a good place to be, as far as he could tell. He could work at his drawing table late into the night, even past midnight if he wished, and beachcomb all afternoon, especially on weekdays when the Salisbury Beach State Reservation was mostly deserted. His room on the second floor of the big, old house gave him privacy. In the town of Salisbury Beach, he had access to a wonderful bakery, some fine eating establishments, and entertainment at the amusement park. Still it was far from busy Boston streets, honking taxis, and the pressure that wore at him most of the year.

On one of those late nights, fully awake and working at his desk, he glanced out a side window. He saw something very strange. He thought it was a soft blue light glowing in the window of the second floor of the house next door, directly across the yard from his own window.

Ken knew about soft blue lights and their historic connection with the presence of ghosts. He had read Shakespeare and was familiar with the expression "Great Caesar's ghost!" He knew that a blue light, whether from a candle flame or other source, was supposed to hint that a ghost was calling. Not sure what was going on next door, or whether he might have been seeing a reflection of some other light, he said nothing about it. He didn't want to upset anyone, especially the owner of the house where he was living, who lived on the first floor.

The next evening, remembering the blue light he had seen the previous night, Ken looked toward the neighboring house again as he finished a long day at his drawing table. He said, "That second night, I thought I saw two blue lights, each in a separate window but, again, on the second floor of that house next door. In the morning, I said nothing, except to ask the landlady if any lights should be on next door. She said, 'Only a white light at the side door.'"

Then the woman leaned toward him and whispered, "It's such a shame," before trotting off to answer a ringing phone.

Only then did Ken notice that the house next door was roped off with yellow police tape as the scene of a crime. Certainly, no one should be in there. But if anyone had sneaked by the barricades, they wouldn't likely draw attention to themselves by turning on lights at night.

Ken observed that on the third night, the blue lights again appeared next door, but through the downstairs back kitchen window. Whatever or whoever was behind their appearance, a slow thorough search of the house seemed to be in progress, first upstairs, now down-stairs. Ken wondered: Would the lights approach the front door next, and exit? Where would they go next?

While picking up cinnamon rolls the next morning at his favorite bakery, he heard talk about that house next door and why it was cordoned off by the police. The man and woman chatting about it said that a murder had taken place there just recently. Those who had heard about it thought the victim, who had lived alone, was named Neville, or Nevins, or some-thing like that. No one was sure. The woman thought he had been killed, "all for the paltry sum of five dollars, the amount in his wallet at the time."

Ken said, "I decided to play 'half-wit Van Helsing.' On the fourth day, I stealthily made my way, unnoticed, through a side yard between the two houses. I approached the side door of the seemingly haunted house. Having heard, by then, about the murder and the supposed motive, I placed a five dollar bill on the welcome mat. All I had with me to weigh it down was a plastic crucifix. I thought, Since that was supposedly the original amount stolen from the deceased, it might put an end to the puzzle, somehow.

"On the fourth night, no blue lights appeared at the windows. Was it over?

"On the fifth day, I checked at the side door. The crucifix was still there, but the five dollar bill wasn't. Maybe the wind took it. Maybe

. . .

"I picked up the crucifix and went back to my rooms. Reflecting later on what had happened, I thought it was as if the ghost had been running up a light bill, and my fiver went toward paying it. At least, I never saw the blue lights again in those windows."

◄ 28 ►

Home and Happy, at Last

A woman named Mary had sat down as Ken was finishing up his story. She gave a visible shudder and offered to tell us a story she had exerienced. We eagerly accepted.

Mary, who hailed from Rochester, Minnesota, began on a happy note. "When Grandmother hugged me on my wedding night," Mary said, "my mind went back to my childhood. I was a young girl in pigtails again. And there was Grandma, much younger, in her print house dress, in her own kitchen, pouring me a glass of milk while I reached into her big apple cookie jar."

When Grandpa congratulated Mary, the vivid vision passed. But for just a minute, Mary had been very close to her grandmother.

After she married, that feeling stayed. Mary and her grandmother remained very close. Not just good friends, or the usual we'll-get-along-because-we're-relatives relationship—much more. She was important to Mary, and Mary felt that she meant something to her grandmother. They enjoyed their special closeness.

After their marriage, Mary and her husband quickly started their family, the first child being born just over a year later. The next year, they had their second child. While Mary was pregnant the third time, her grandmother had a stroke.

Mary said, "I was surprised . . . even crushed. How could this happen to me?" She felt that Grandma should be there for her forever.

Mary said later, "The stroke left Grandma with problems, but she was soon able to communicate well enough to let the family know what her one and only wish was. She whispered, 'All I want is to live long enough to see my third great-grandchild.'

"Our son, our third child," Mary went on with a bittersweet smile, "was born on October 11. Grandmother did get to see him. In fact, shortly after he was born, she came to stay with us for a while.

"She stayed on through the holidays, adding a special touch of warmth and spirit to our lives. But she had to either stay with us longer or go back to her home. Traveling back and forth was as hard on her as going up and down our stairs was.

"Much as I hated to see her leave, Grandmother went back to her own home about the second week of January. I could see she didn't want to go, but Grandfather insisted. I think I knew as well as he did that three young children under three years of age and an eighty-nine-year-old woman who could hardly walk did not make a good combination for an overworked young mother. Besides, she was blind in one eye, which didn't make it any easier for her or for me. But I guess I hoped I could hang onto her a little longer.

"Grandpa won out. Grandmother returned home.

"After Grandmother left, I visited her. Every day, I took the babies along to her house several blocks over, made her lunch, and put the kids down for naps. Then the two of us sat and talked. I never questioned how Grandpa or my own family felt about that. It was just something that seemed natural for me to do. Grandmother had been part of my life since my girlhood, and I think I wanted it to stay that way.

"On January 23, the call came. Grandmother had died that day. We buried her a few days later. It was over, or so I thought.

"Can you believe that for six months after her death, I continued to dress my children and take them along to Grandmother's house, to the grandmother who was no no longer there? Sure, Grandpa was there, and we visited, and I made him his lunch just as I had done before, but I actually wasn't there for him. He was my step-grandfather; Grandmother and he had married well after I had been born, so I never really thought of him in the same way I had thought of old Grandpa Joe, her first husband.

No, I went there for Grandmother. It seemed that I felt some sort of compulsion to go to her, to spend time with her. I often would not remember until I reached the front door that she was not there. It happened day after day. It was as though a void in my life left me unable to cope reasonably with her death, my great loss.

"About six months after Grandmother's death, two of my friends and I were standing on a street corner in Rochester. Someone tapped me on the shoulder.

"It was a clear day in July. Sunny and bright and midday. But when I turned, there stood my grandmother. Her loving smile and her beautiful, gray-white hair were the same. She was wearing the blue lace dress she was buried in.

"I knew I wasn't imagining this because my two friends also saw her.

"All she said was, 'Would you please give me some money to get home?'

"I don't know what I gave her—coins, bills—but I dug into my purse immediately and pulled something out. I handed over something. As soon as I did, she disappeared.

"My friends and I went in different directions to different bus stops. Nothing more happened. But something was different for me. I couldn't believe what had happened just then. I had no doubt it was Grandmother who had appeared. I've had to accept that it was her spirit. And she was so real that I did as she asked, helped her as I was always willing to do.

"After that day, I never ended up at her house believing she was there. I visited Grandpa, sure, but it was different. I went to see him. I truly believe Grandmother came that day to let me know that she was home and was fine."

◄ 29 ►

Cipher

I was camping at Itasca State Park, the headwaters of the Mississippi River. It was not unusual to find people from all over the country at this park, especially people from much farther down the great river. At Itasca, a person could easily walk stepping stones across what amounted to a brisk little stream that flowed out of a large marshy area. This was the baby Mississippi that would grow into Old Man River hundreds of miles to the south.

In response to my usual notice on the camp bulletin board, Audrey of St. Charles, Missouri, and her husband, Neil, joined my campfire and told their haunting story.

They were visiting their daughter's home in Clinton, Pennsylvania. "The house," Audrey said, "was over a hundred years old and at one time, had been a stagecoach station."

Audrey had slept in the house and in the same bedroom many times during their visits over a period of years. Though nothing unexplainable had ever happened before, the first night of this particular visit turned out to be another story.

Looking forward to a good night's sleep after a long trip and a hectic day, Audrey snuggled down and relaxed. But not for long. After just a minute or two, her flashlight on the night stand turned on. Hardly asleep yet, she became alert enough to reach over and turn it off. She was just about all snuggled in again when she heard a male voice she didn't recognize. It sounded like an elderly man. Though she had no idea as to who or why, she heard the voice reciting numbers . . . for example, "one plus five, plus three, minus six, CIPHER. Four plus six, minus three, plus seven, CIPHER." Each time she heard a series of numbers, she heard the word "cipher" at the end of the formula or whatever it was.

When Audrey, without even looking toward where the voice came from, said, "Shut up!" the voice stopped immediately. She said later, "I am not a rude person, but I was exhausted. All I wanted at the moment was to get some sleep. I felt no fear. I slept then, but in the morning I felt remorse for my rudeness. Whoever 'he' was, he had been very polite. As I became fully awake in the morning, I tried to make sense out of what had happened. The series of numbers with the 'plus' and the 'minus' directions didn't even add up to a cipher, if he meant cipher as nothing or zero as the end result."

The more she thought about it, the more puzzled she became. At first, she had thought of "cipher" as meaning "nothing," "naught," "zero." But computing the series of numbers along with the addition and subtraction directives didn't add up to zero. The dictionary gave another meaning: a nonentity. As relating to the ghost, if it was one, that sort of made sense. But, again, what about the plus and minus? Another meaning admitted the possibility of a code, as in secret writing, but Audrey had heard it as it was spoken. And again, what did the pluses and the minuses mean? Thinking about that made Audrey wonder if maybe . . . back when the old house was still a stagecoach station . . . maybe an elderly mathematician had died there. Maybe the voice was his and his spirit somehow stuck there all this time.

Three days after the incident, in the early afternoon, Audrey was lying on the bed with a heating pad around her neck because it was stiff. Her husband came to the bedroom door and said, "Audrey, I'm going to take a shower. Here's Josh." Then he put their pet Doberman in the room with Audrey and closed the door.

Josh lay down on the floor at the foot of the bed. Audrey said, "All was peaceful, and I could relax. Suddenlly Josh jumped up, snarling and growling, and attacked something next to the bed. Almost immediately, he turned and ran to the door, all the while whining and crying, making it clear that he wanted out of that room right now. All the while, I had my eyes wide open, but I saw nothing unusual . . . no one was in the room but Josh and me. The dog was usually a very calm, evenly-tempered Doberman. That was the only time I ever heard him growl and attack. Nevertheless, after that incident, the dog wouldn't go near that room again."

About two weeks after their visit ended, Audrey's daughter Nancy had some unexpected callers. They were the previous residents of the house. As they talked, the lady asked Nancy, "Did you have any strange things happen to you while you were living here?"

Nancy hesitated to talk about what had happened, so first she asked the caller the same question. The woman proceeded to tell her about hearing an old man saying some sequences of numbers, followed by the word "cipher."

Nancy was baffled. She couldn't figure out any explanation, even as she talked with this previous occupant who had had an experience very similar to hers. Their conversation shed no light on the subject at all, so when Audrey next heard from Nancy, she learned nothing new. But Audrey did an oil painting of "the ghost" in the same bedroom where she had met up with it, and gave the painting to her daughter. But when Nancy showed it to others, she asked, "How could Mother do that? She painted a representation of nothing! She never even saw anything there when she heard that voice!"

Audrey said, "No, I never saw the old man whose voice recited the cipher, but I have a memory of him."

When I and others around the campfire questioned her about this, she just shook her head. "I have a memory of someone I never saw. I know how this sounds, but it's true. The next morning, I easily remembered the voice in the room and knew for fact that I had seen nothing. But I had this image of the man anyway. I can't explain it."

Neither could we.

⊰ 30 ⊱

A House to Be Avoided

Judy, from Knoxville, Tennessee, had come up to Itasca State Park as the beginning of a trip the entire length of the Mississippi. She thought starting at the beginning just made good sense. As it turned out, she had a passion for ghost stories and weird happenings, some of which stemmed from her own childhood, and she shared one with us.

Judy was a grandchild of Frank Cooper and his wife, Nellie, who had had eight children. Judy remembers incidents from when the family lived in an old Victorian house in the west side of Indianapolis, Indiana, that led to their belief that the house had a ghost.

Built in the 1890s, the big house had two stories plus an attic. It also had a fruit cellar, but, strange as it may seem, that damp, creepy space wasn't significant in Judy's story. Incidents that led the Cooper family to believe the house hosted a ghost always happened in the attic.

In the 1920s, when they lived in that particular house, it had already seen a number of renters. The Coopers lived in the house longer than any other family, Judy said. "The people who rented it before Grandpa did only stayed a week before moving out. After Grandpa, the next family only stayed in the house a grand total of two weeks."

It would seem, then, that the owner had trouble renting the house out or keeping it occupied. That was probably because folks around there believed it was haunted, and they did everything they could to avoid any contact with it. They always crossed the street when walking down that block, instead of going right past it on the same side of the street. And the kids in the neighborhood avoided it entirely.

Some people heard noises there, such as moaning, crying, or heavy footsteps. The Cooper kids heard footsteps when they were in their bedrooms. Those kids were Judy's father and his siblings. When that kind of thing happened, they always sent one of the kids—usually the eldest—down to the first floor where their parents slept, "to get Grandpa," Judy said. "Grandpa would come upstairs and check, but he'd never find anything there—at least, nothing he could see—that caused the noises they had heard, and resulted in their being afraid."

Judy recalled her grandmother's reaction on those occasions. "Grandma," Judy said, "who had been born and raised in Knoxville, Tennessee, and was of Cherokee descent, wouldn't get into it at all. She always said, 'Leave it alone.' Now that I understand the ways of her people better than I did then, I sometimes wonder if she believed a spirit was causing the incidents. If so, she would respect the spirit instead of suspecting it or disturbing it."

Eventually, the Cooper family was forced to move out, reportedly for an entirely different reason than the house's unseen occupants: Grandpa felt that the old style gas lights weren't safe with young, rambunctious kids around. He wanted electric lights, but the owner wouldn't modernize the lighting system, so the family moved out.

The house, still standing in west Indianapolis at the time of this writing, is also still occupied. Judy didn't know whether the present occupants were aware of these earlier happenings. She thought they might not be because she found out that when the owner died, the hauntings stopped.

Judy said, "The people who moved in about a week after Grandpa and Grandma Cooper and their family moved out found a big blood stain—deep burgundy—on the attic floorboards. It's no wonder they didn't stay longer than two weeks! We learned that the man who originally had the house built had killed his wife with an ax up in the attic! No matter who we talked to, or where we searched in the earlier newspapers and death records, we never did find out if this was true. What we did learn was that, for many years, the earlier owner couldn't keep it rented. Apparently too many strange, scary things happened that didn't fit the character of an old, elegant Victorian house. And when people don't understand something, they find it easy to avoid or, in Grandma Cooper's words, to simply 'Leave it alone!'"

⊰ 31 ⊱

Unusual Patterns in the Carpet

Being a devotee of ghost stories, Judy had a second story to tell. After her father married, her parents bought a brick house in Plainfield, Indiana. That was in 1979 or 1980. The house had been built by a doctor for his wife, but she died before it was finished, so she never had the pleasure of living in it.

When Judy's father and mother were considering the purchase, and they went to look at the house, Judy's mother thought it strange that there were slide-bolt locks on the inside of the doors from the bedroom to the outdoors. She didn't ask the real estate agent about it until after they moved in, but she sure wondered about it.

When she did get around to asking about the locks, she was told that the real estate agent and her family had lived in the house for a time. While there, they had put the locks on because the realtor was afraid of the ghost—the "bumps in the night" that she hadn't been told about by the former owner. Later, the woman explained, she found out that no one had ever lived in that house more than three or four years. No wonder she had the locks put on, and no wonder she was eager to sell the house to another prospect.

But Judy's parents purchased the house nonetheless and prepared to move in. Judy recalled, "Mom had new carpeting laid in the living room and hallway right away, so it was brand new. Then they settled in and were just starting to feel comfortable, when Mom became aware of something very strange going on. She noticed that at about the same time every evening, she could see an arc shape that the bottom edge of the front door made in the nap of the new carpeting. That wouldn't have seemed so strange, except for the fact that no one had just come in—no one of the family members or anyone they could see. They could also feel the rush of air that would be normal if someone had opened the door and come in, and they could see footprints in the new carpeting. They made a beeline to the hall closet. They could also see the arc pattern where the closet door would swing open as if someone opened it, and then hear a thud as if someone set something fairly heavy down in the closet. Next they would feel the rush of air again, as if the front door opened and closed, and then they heard the footsteps again, as if someone walked to the bedroom."

Judy said, "Believe me, if I had been there, I wouldn't have followed those footsteps into the bedroom for anything. You couldn't have paid me to do that. And I was almost forty when I heard about all this."

Judy went on the tell about another episode. She said, "In that same house, the basement was finished off and had sleeping quarters down there. Once, I was lying on one of the beds, when suddenly I heard footsteps approaching. I didn't move. I figured it was Dad or Mom coming down for something. The sounds came to a stop at the head of the bed where I lay quietly with my eyes closed. I waited for Dad or Mom to say something. When they didn't, I looked up and—well, it wasn't either of them, but there definitely was someone or something there. It was a figure—like the silhouette of a man—sort of smoky gray. I just stared. I didn't move, though. I soon heard the footsteps as 'it' went back upstairs. Maybe this visage had just come down there to check on me, to see what I was doing there. I just don't know.

"Anyway, when I told Dad and Mom about this, they both had a good laugh. They were well aware of their ghost. They had heard the footsteps for years. And when they heard me tearing up the stairs, really freaked, all they could do was laugh. They must have accepted the ghost in that house and felt comfortable with it all the time—even Mom!

"One night, Tom and I and our four kids spent the night at Grandpa and Grandma's. The kids loved to do that. They called these their 'famous slumber parties at Grandma's.' On that particular night, two of them were sleeping on the floor. The other two lay on the hide-a-bed Grandma had made up for them. That night, there was a moment when Theresa felt a cold breeze. She shivered and told Grandma. Grandma said, 'Oh, just forget it. It'll pass.'

"Before long, John, Suzanne, and Jim complained, too. Grandma still just laughed. She said, 'Didn't you see the door open?' Then she said, 'Wait. You'll feel it again.' And they did. 'The closet door opened,' she said. By now, the kids are all huddled together in the same bed, and pretty scared. The door didn't actually open, but they could see the arc pattern in the carpeting. Then she told them to listen for the thump in the closet. They were very quiet then, and they heard the thump. Later, they figured out that the thump was the sound made when the doctor who originally had the house built returned home from the day's work and set his bag down in the closet before he headed for the bedroom to get his suit off and dress more comfortably."

Judy gave a little laugh. "That's all our ghost did, come in, drop off his bag and head upstairs. Must be boring to do the same things over and over and over."

‹ 32 ›

Whose Ghosts Haunt the Courthouse?

Up to now, a woman sitting near my campfire had been pretty quiet, listening to the stories being told. Her expression had been one of rapt attention as she followed the tales told by different speakers. But after Judy's story, when no one else offered a new ghost story, she suddenly seemed to come awake as though she had a story to tell us. The rest of us encouraged her, Mel, to tell us what she knew.

Although Mel hailed from Montana, she had been to the Atlantic County Courthouse in Mays Landing, New Jersey, on a trip visiting family. Stories about the old courthouse being haunted abounded, Mel told us. "Even the president of the Atlantic County Historical Society had agreed with those who said that the courthouse was haunted," she said. Mel's daughter, who lived in Mays Landing, had heard many stories about the building's ghosts. Though she had never seen one herself, several reliable employees had told of their experiences.

One was a sheriff's officer who, with a co-worker, heard someone crying as the two opened the building one morning. The crying seemed to come from a courtroom. When they checked that room, they both saw a shadowy woman trying to comfort a crying child in one corner. Neither the woman nor the child responded to offers of help, and when the officers turned on the lights, no one was there. This crying was also heard by several others over many years.

Courthouse workers heard a woman crying one afternoon while they were chatting together in a courtroom. When they called a sheriff's officer to check on this, he heard the sounds but found no one. Those who first heard the mysterious woman said, "She sounded like an older woman, and she was crying real hard."

One clerk was leaving the building about 6:30 p.m. one stormy evening, when she heard a woman crying outside of the courtroom door. As soon as she touched the doorknob, the crying stopped and was replaced by singing. No one could be seen anywhere outside the courthouse that night . . . not even a homeless woman who had often hung around and was presumed, for a time, to be the person crying.

Three workers heard keys rattling in a hallway late one night. The three brave souls searched the hallway, looking for an intruder, but no one was there. At least, no one they could see.

One of the strangest incidents, Mel told us, took place in the early 1980s. Two employees, working late one night, suddenly heard a loud buzzing near the ceiling. The pitch of the sound kept changing from high to low and back again. That ruled out the possibility of it being a smoke alarm. It also seemed to be moving around just below the drop ceiling.

One of the workers had been on the phone. She quickly hung up and rushed from the room. The other person, one of the clerks, climbed onto a desk and reached toward the ceiling. She turned very white and said, "I felt air movement. It moved right past my hand." She said. "That was enough for me. I got out of there as fast as I could."

In about 1990, the same clerk was making photocopies after hours, up on the second floor. When a sheriff's officer ran past her with his hand on his gun, she didn't know what to think and poked her head out the door to watch him gallop down the hall. He told her later, "I'd been turning off the lights in Courtroom Two, the oldest room in the building, but every time I did and came back to check, they'd be on again. I thought maybe we had a prowler, but no one was there. It was really spooky."

Usually the elevators at the Atlantic County Courthouse only ran when someone pushed the UP or the DOWN buttons. Otherwise, they didn't run. But on some nights, employees would still hear the elevator, and no one had pushed the buttons. And that wasn't all. Doors were often heard closing again behind someone such as the custodian who had just closed them as he made his rounds. And footsteps were heard in halls and rooms where no one was working. People woudd see lights going on and off.

Then Mel's eyes grew very large. She whispered, "My daughter took me to the courthouse just to see the place because she knew I liked ghost stories. It was late in the day, after the courts had emptied. I stopped in the ladies' room. I washed my hands and turned off the faucet. Before I reached for a paper towel, the old faucet creaked back on. I turned it off again and watched. In a moment, it creaked back on. That was it for me. I was out of there so fast, my daughter had to run to catch me."

Whose spirits haunt the old Atlantic County Courthouse at Mays Landing? Some assert that these are the spirits of people hanged from the hanging tree that once stood just outside the courthouse. One might be the ghost of the man who hanged himself in the building's bell tower. Another could be the spirit of the would-be thief who tried to pry open the safe in the bookkeeping office but died of a heart attack in the process or the ghost of someone lurking in the title-search department, trying to prevent the employees from stumbling onto a deep, dark secret in the early records. No one knows for sure.

◄ 33 ►

Their Ghost Caught Up with Them

I met Barbara at Crow Wing State Park in east-central Minnesota near the Wisconsin border. We were chatting with each other from adjacent campsites, and I mentioned that I had several books published with ghost stories. Right then and there, Barbara came through the wild raspberries that separated our sites and sat down. Her expression was deep fascination. She, of course, had a story to tell.

Barbara and her family lived in a large house in St. Cloud, Minnesota, for six or seven years before they realized they had a ghost "living" with them there. Barbara said, "It came on gradually. Different ones of us would notice little things, and finally we compared notes and realized there was something unusual going on there.

"At first, it seemed as though someone was playing pranks on us, such as turning over all the toothbrushes in the holder. One morning, all the toothbrushes were wet.

"Whoever or whatever was responsible, another thing it did was to throw a handful of pennies behind the toilet in the basement every once in a while. I just kept vacuuming them up.

"For a while, it would take all the safety pins out of the pincushion, but leave the stickpins there. Later, I'd find all the safety pins, unexpectedly, in a pile somewhere else, like a drawer in the dining room or a sock in the basement.

"It hid a Christmas watch before I could wrap it. The next summer, I found the watch on my shelf of empty fruit jars. I would never have taken the watch down into the basement with me.

"One day, I ran home from work for a sandwich at lunchtime. While I was sitting in the living room eating it and watching TV, a *National Geographic Magazine* jumped off the coffee table and onto the floor. And it hadn't even been close to the edge of the coffee table.

"Sometimes the hangers I'd hung on a door casing as I was ironing would suddenly dance and jiggle, and there was no way to explain why.

"When noises came from storage shelves behind me as I loaded the washing machine, I would say, 'Knock it off!' and the noises would stop. And, even though it was an older home, we've never had mice in that house.

"By the fact that it pulled these pranks and hid things where I would never expect to find them, I wondered sometimes if we had a poltergeist. One time it took all the kitchen knives and hid them under the dust ruffle of my bedskirt. Other kitchen items were eventually found up on top shelves in the kids' toy room. I could tell by the looks on the girls' faces when I questioned them that they weren't the ones responsible.

"Rented videos were sometimes hidden so that, as a result, we had to pay fines. Later, the videos would show up in the bathroom sink. For a while we stopped renting movies as a result. Once, all of my daughter Julie's underwear was hidden behind the wood furnace in the basement. I eventually found her things, but by then mildew had attacked them and I'd had to replace them.

"At one point, the strange presence in the house started talking. It seemed to enjoy calling to a member of the family to come to a certain place, like, 'Amy, come get a cookie,' or, 'Come upstairs now, Julie.' We would respond only to find no reason or person who had called.

"The dog sat up once and pricked up its ears while it looked at me as if to say, What was that?" when it heard what had to be the ghost sneezing in the basement. As far as I know, dogs only hear *real* things, so it wasn't imagined.

"Julie, my oldest, moved to an apartment across town at one point. She thinks it may have moved with her. Once, when her bedroom door was locked, the doorknob jerked wildly as if someone was trying to get in. Scared, she had to telephone a friend to come over, let herself in, and find out who or what was outside her bedroom door. When the friend came, there was no sign that anyone had been there. Once, it sounded like a raccoon was in Julie's closet, ripping her clothes to shreds. She called her dad to check it out. That was at two a.m. There was nothing unusual in the closet when he came to check it.

"After that night, Julie decided to take control of her own life. She ordered the entity to leave her alone, so then she had more peace of mind for a while.

"Although Julie seemed to be the one the ghost favored at first, once Julie moved on, the ghost attached itself to Sarah, my middle daughter, during her later high school years. When she was a junior in high school, it actually took on the appearance of a greenish, glowing light in one corner of her room. It wouldn't leave its corner for a long time. That was really upsetting, and we couldn't figure out what to do about it so that Sarah would feel more secure.

"One day when we were talking about the ghost, Sarah reminded me of the scariest situation she had ever found herself in. One night, the ghost woke her by shaking her bed violently for about thirty seconds. She told me, 'Mom, I was so terrified that I couldn't even scream. The bed jumped six to eight inches up and down.'

"Julie thinks our ghost was back at her apartment recently. She said that a large picture over the sofa started to rattle, jump around and pull out from the wall several inches before it crashed to the floor. She wasn't even home at the time, but her two roommates were there and saw it, and they were terrified when Julie told them what she thought might have been responsible.

"There came a time when we all just figured we'd had enough, so we sold that house and moved into a smaller one in another part of town. But it may have followed us. In just the last few weeks, it's taken to turning photos around so that they aren't facing us as we enter a room or look toward a photo. But maybe there's a little improvement. It doesn't seem to have a voice now. It doesn't call out to us, or, at least, it hasn't yet. But I do sense movement in the rooms upstairs, and sometimes that sensation is pretty powerful."